Tabitha Plimtock

AND THE
Edge of the
World

Erika McGann grew up in Drogheda, County Louth, and now lives in Dublin. She is the author of a number of children's books, including the winner of the Waverton Good Read Children's Award 2014, *The Demon Notebook*, the first in her magical series about Grace and her four friends, which also includes *The Broken Spell*, *The Watching Wood* and *The Midnight Carnival*. She is the author of the 'Cass and the Bubble Street Gang' series and of four picture books, *Where Are You, Puffling?*, *Puffling and the Egg* and *Wee Donkey's Treasure Hunt*, all illustrated by Gerry Daly, and *The Night-time Cat and the Plump, Grey Mouse*, illustrated by Lauren O'Neill.

Phillip Cullen grew up in Dublin and studied classical animation at Ballyfermot College. He loves to draw cute, weird and wonderful creatures. After a period living in Japan he now lives in Dublin with his wife.

Tabitha Plimtock

Plimtock

AND THE
Edge of the
World

Erika McGann

illustrated by Phillip Cullen

THE O'BRIEN PRESS
DUBLIN

For Marek,

for being kind and generous, and always supportive

Acknowledgements

I'd like to thank Phillip Cullen for his gorgeously brilliant illustrations of Tabitha and the world at the edge; they have added so much to the book. My fabulous editor, Nicola Reddy, for such a fun and easy edit. Mary-Lou McCarthy for her endless support, and my family for all their encouragement.

I'd also like to thank designer Emma Byrne, Aoife Harrison (a.k.a. Harri), Ruth Heneghan, Tríona Marshall, Brenda Boyne, and everyone at The O'Brien Press.

First published 2021 by
The O'Brien Press Ltd,
12 Terenure Road East, Rathgar,
Dublin 6, D06 HD27, Ireland.
Tel: +353 1 4923333; Fax: +353 1 4922777
E-mail: books@obrien.ie
Website: www.obrien.ie
The O'Brien Press is a member of Publishing Ireland.

ISBN: 978-1-78849-249-2
Text © copyright Erika McGann 2021
The moral rights of the author have been asserted.
Copyright for typesetting, layout, editing, design
© The O'Brien Press Ltd
Design and layout by Emma Byrne
Illustrations by Phillip Cullen

1 3 5 7 8 6 4 2
21 23 25 24 22

Printed and bound by Norhaven Paperback A/S, Denmark.
The paper in this book is produced using pulp from managed forests.

Tabitha Plimtock and the Edge of the World receives
financial assistance from the Arts Council. The
Author also wishes to thank the Arts Council for
the bursary which allowed her to write this book.

Published in
DUBLIN
UNESCO
City of Literature

Contents

CHAPTER ONE

THE HOUSE AT THE EDGE OF THE WORLD

I know what you're thinking. You read the title above and thought it must be a metaphor. There is no edge of the world; every scientist (and every non-scientist) knows that. The earth is round. If you try to reach the edge of it, you'll just keep going and going.

And yes, you're right, the earth is round. And if you start walking from, say, Paris, and keep walking (and sailing, or swimming), you'll eventually come right back to Paris again. And again, and again. But if you circle the world enough times (say, eleven or twelve or thirteen times) you will, I promise you, reach the edge of the world. And it is an actual edge. A drop-off. A great big cliff. The world is there, all solid and sensible, and then all of a sudden it's not. The ground just ends.

There's not much at the edge of the world, as you can imagine. It takes an awfully long time to get there, so most people don't bother, and it hasn't got much in the way of trees and grass and soil to grow things in. By the time you near the edge of the world, there's little left of the ground but rock. So it's a rocky, slightly dusty, place.

But it's not entirely lacking in people. There is one house there – teetering on the very edge of that great big cliff – and in it are the five permanent residents who make up the Plimtock family.

Bertha Plimtock is by far the eldest. She's one-hundred-and-something years old, or even older, maybe two-hundred-and-something. No-one knows exactly because no-one else in the house was alive when she was born. Not even Bertha's sure how old she is, but she is certain of her birthday. It's today. I don't mean the sixteenth of May, or the fifth of December, or whatever day you happen to be reading this story. I mean it's *today*. Every day is, at some point, today, so every day is Bertha's birthday.

Bertha lives in a room on the ground floor – what would be the sitting room in most houses – sitting on a giant beanbag with a party hat on, waiting impatiently for her birthday cake and presents. The other members of the family take turns baking the cake. Some days it's a lemon drizzle cake, some days it's chocolate fudge. Some days it's a black forest gateau and some days it's a Victoria sponge. On bad days it's a healthy, seed-filled bran cake with soya yoghurt instead of icing. Bertha's usual foul mood gets even worse on those days.

Gower Plimtock is the one who makes the healthy cakes. Gower is Bertha's eldest grandchild. He's fussy and mean, and he spends most of his time in the kitchen, lecturing people about the evils of sugar and dairy, or in the front garden, jogging on the spot.

After Gower, there's Gristle. She's the opposite of her brother. She likes a mess. Correction, she *loves* a mess. Gristle is the type of person who will hide outside the door as you clean the bathroom, then, just as the sink reaches the point where it's gleaming and shiny, she'll spring into the room and squirt shampoo all over the tiles.

Cousin Wilbur has a long-burning, smouldering temper, which might be in part because he suffers from a very strange affliction. When the wind blows from east to west he's perfectly normal (or as perfectly normal as any of the Plimtock family can be), but when the wind blows from west to east he becomes an animal.

You didn't misread that; he, in fact, turns into an animal. I know you find that difficult to believe – it's not a common ailment in most places on the

planet, like measles or chickenpox – but it is a con-
dition that plagues people at the edge of the world.
Something to do with humidity levels and exposure
to non-world air. Anyway, Wilbur caught it when he
was very young and never quite recovered. The type
of animal he turns into depends on the composition
of the wind – dry winds tend to bring on bouts of
chameleon or armadillo, sandy winds cause eruptions
of meerkat or camel, a cold wind can make him break
out in an arctic fox, a penguin or even, once, a polar
bear. And salty winds … well, you get the idea.

You would think that Cousin Wilbur would be the
more intriguing of the Plimtocks, but personally I
think the youngest in the family is by far the most
interesting. I say 'in the family', but the others don't
really think of her as family. They think of her more
like an ox or a mule or a horse that pulls a plough; a
working farm animal is what I mean. She's a useful
thing that they keep around because she's … well,
useful.

Tabitha Plimtock is a mystery. In the same way nobody knows exactly how old Bertha Plimtock is, nobody knows exactly how Tabitha Plimtock came to be. Oh, they all *remember* how she arrived at the house. The only problem is they all *remember* something totally different.

'Dumped in a basket on the doorstep,' Gower Plimtock says. 'What was it, eight years ago? Nine? Doorbell rang and there the little snot was.'

'No, no,' Gristle disagrees, 'she crawled out of the pond just over yonder. Saw it myself. Like a greasy lizard, covered in slime. Scared the life out of me.'

'Rubbish,' Cousin Wilbur (at this moment a stick insect) says. 'She was dropped from an airplane, I was there. Someone yelled, "Here, keep it, we don't want it!", and the thing landed at my feet like an elephant's turd.'

When asked, Bertha Plimtock just says, 'Who?'

The reason Tabitha Plimtock is so very useful is because she's a go-getter. Now you probably think

I mean she's an achiever, someone who's successful – and maybe someday she will be – but a go-getter in the house at the edge of the world is more like a dogsbody. A person to go and get things. A go-getter.

'Tabitha, go get some eggs.'

'Tabitha, go get some pumpkin seeds.'

'Tabitha, go get the newspaper.'

Do you see what I mean?

I'll be happy to tell you more about Tabitha Plimtock and the edge of the world – much more – but I think that's quite enough for one chapter. You probably need a little break to take in what you've read so far, so grab yourself a cup of tea and a biscuit, have a breather, and I'll see you in Chapter Two.

THE NET

Now that you've had a few moments to process the information you've received so far, I'm sure you have some questions. Like, how can Tabitha go and get pumpkin seeds when the edge of the world is mostly rock? Where do the pumpkins grow? And where do the Plimtocks get flour for birthday cakes if there are no farmers to grow wheat and no soil to grow the wheat in? Well, okay, I did mislead you a little there, because I'm trying to introduce this place one bit at a time – it would be too complicated otherwise. The fact is that there is more to the edge of the world than one house on a rocky ledge. There's a forest inland with too few trees, for example, and a tavern some miles away where goods are bartered and traded. But for Tabitha, the rest of the edge is accessible via the net.

The net hangs from the roof off the back of the Plimtocks' house, spilling down the cliff like a green veil for as far as the eye can see. It's not made of rope or plastic, but of vines. At some point in history, a bunch of vines sprouted from between the roof tiles of the house, criss-crossed each other as they grew, and then just kept on growing.

The cliff face is where Tabitha spends most of her time. Every day she steps out onto the window-sill of her first-floor bedroom, wiggles through the green lattice, and climbs down the outside of the net. When I say Tabitha's *bedroom*, I mean *bath-room*. It's a three-bedroom house – Gower, Gristle and Cousin Wilbur each have a bedroom and Bertha has the front room downstairs, which leaves only the bathroom for Tabitha. She sleeps in the bath with a rolled-up jumper for a pillow. The shower curtain around the bath offers a little privacy, but she still gets a fright anytime someone gets up to use the toilet in the middle of the night.

Anyway, back to the net and Tabitha climbing down the cliff wall. The cliff is rocky but full of holes, like stony Swiss cheese. These holes are generally referred to as 'wall pockets'. Some wall pockets are empty, some of them have insects and moss and other things growing in them, and some of them have people living in them. The people tend to live in the bigger, nicer wall pockets, the ones with natural air-conditioning (provided by cracks in the rock) or running water (provided by other cracks in the rock) or stony balconies. And they grow things from seeds that blow in on the prevailing winds from places all over the world, and they raise animals too: chickens (or things like chickens) and ducks and geese (or things quite like ducks and geese). The animals at the edge of the world have been evolving on their own for centuries, for millennia, so they're a little different to the animals you and I know, but for the sake of simplicity

I'll refer to them as chickens and ducks and geese, etc.

On this particular morning, Tabitha wakes to the distant sound of a cockerel crowing (he lives in a wall pocket some way down the cliff). The sun has just risen and it's very early. She unrolls her jumper-pillow and puts it on over her t-shirt as a jumper-jumper. Then she hurries downstairs and turns the oven on to preheat. It's Tuesday, so it's Tabitha's turn to make Bertha's birthday cake, and she's planning to do a cherry and almond one with white icing. She hums a lively tune as she pours sugar on top of the butter and starts whipping. As she whips with one hand, she reaches out to put a tick by her name on the birthday cake roster, which looks like this:

Monday – Gower

Tuesday – Tabitha

Wednesday – Gristle

Thursday – Tabitha

Friday – Wilbur

Saturday – Tabitha

… and since Sunday is everybody's day off:

Sunday – Tabitha

'I hope you're using the low-fat butter.' Gower is standing in the kitchen doorway, straightening the sweatbands on his forehead and wrists.

'Yes,' Tabitha replies.

'Well, you little snot, you shouldn't be using butter at all. Are you trying to kill Granny? My poor dear Granny?'

'No, Gower, I swear I'm not. I'm keeping it as healthy as I can, but you know she loves this recipe.'

Gower is already gone. Through the open front door Tabitha can see him jogging on the spot, lifting his knees up very high. She's not sure he cares at all about his precious Granny, but he does like to give out first thing in the morning. It's part of his work-out, which will continue for most of the day.

'Sssssstupid child,' says a slithery voice that makes Tabitha jump.

She looks around and finally spots a blue-coloured snake curled around the cornicing at the edge of the ceiling.

'Oh, Cousin Wilbur. You gave me a fright.'

The snake lunges and hisses with laughter when she jumps again.

'Ssstupid child,' he says, 'you know cherriesss make old Bertha fart. You're trying to make life missserable for the ressst of usss.'

Tabitha sighs and keeps on stirring.

'I'm not at all, Cousin Wilbur, I'm just trying to bake something she likes because I don't have time to bake another. I've to head down the cliff soon.'

'Yessss, head down the cliff and leave usss with Bertha's gasss. Sssselfish brat.'

Tabitha ignores him as best she can by measuring out the flour and almonds, but while she's turned away the blue snake Wilbur slides his tail around the washing-up liquid bottle and squeezes a big glug of it into the mixture.

Half an hour later and Bertha is screaming for her cake.

'It's my birthday!' she cries. 'And no-one brings me cake or presents. What a horrible, selfish family I have.'

She lounges on her giant beanbag, snapping her party hat on and off her head in agitation.

'Here you are, Bertha,' Tabitha says, rushing in. 'It's cherry and almond with royal icing.'

She plonks the cake down on a little coffee table and quickly lights the three candles stuck in the top.

'And the song,' Bertha squeals. 'Sing the bloody song!'

Tabitha hurriedly sings *Happy Birthday*, while Gower, Gristle and Cousin Wilbur carry in badly wrapped presents. (Bertha's got a dreadful memory, so luckily the family don't have to get new birthday presents every day. They just rewrap the same ones over and over again.)

'Make a wish,' says Gristle.

'Yesss,' grins Cousin Wilbur, 'make a wisshhh.'

Bertha shuts her eyes as she cuts into the cake, then grabs a great big handful and shoves it into her mouth.

'*Pthewww!*' Bits of saliva-soggy cake go flying everywhere and Bertha's round face goes very red. 'What is that?! It tastes like poison. Why have you given me poison?! Killers, murderers! You want my house, you're all trying to finish me off! *Murderers!* And on my *birthday*.'

Tabitha closes her eyes and takes a deep breath. She'll have to make another cake. The wall will have to wait.

CHAPTER THREE

MR OFFAL

Tabitha pauses mid-climb and turns her face up to the sun. It's a lovely day. She's got a long shopping list, and she's already short on time because of the birthday cake debacle, but she takes a moment to enjoy the warmth. The vines contract around her to form a little dent in the net, like a cat's bed, and she nestles in for a cozy rest as the sunshine gently beams down. When a light breeze brushes a few loose hairs across her neck, she's so relaxed she could fall asleep.

Her eyes snap open and she continues her descent. It wouldn't do to fall asleep now – she might loosen her grip and plunge many miles to her death or, even worse, miss out on the shopping and have to return

to the house empty-handed.

Eggs are first on the list, and they're a dangerous one. Mr Offal's wall pocket is some way from the safety of the net, along a hundred metres of treacherous, narrow ledge. Tabitha grips the rough wall with her fingertips, hoping none of it has been infested by rock worms. (They're black worms that grow to only a few centimetres in length, but they have diamond teeth. They chew through stone in spirally patterns, weakening the rock from underneath. It's tough to spot the weak bits, but you'll sometimes see clusters of tiny holes where the worms have popped out to sun themselves.) She slips once and a mini cascade of dust and pebbles goes tumbling down the wall. She tries not to look down and makes it to the wall pocket in one piece.

'Mr Offal?' she says as she grips the edge of the opening in the rock. 'It's me, Tabitha.'

'Heads up, Tabby girl! Blue one from a short-toed webber.'

Tabitha snatches a rolled-up towel from the side of her backpack, and just in time too. As she rounds the corner to the safety of the pocket, something small and blue comes flying at her head. It ricochets off the soft towel and Tabitha dives to catch it before it hits the ground. The pretty little duck egg isn't even cracked.

There's squawking and a flurry of feathers from a pen at the back of the wall pocket. Mr Offal's wide bottom is jammed in the door of the pen as he stoops in amongst the flapping birds.

'A white from a long-toed webber, coming up!' His voice is muffled in the pen. 'Ooh, this is a good one.'

'Hold on, Mr Offal,' Tabitha says, frantically unzipping her backpack, 'just one second.'

She barely has time to pull out a padded box and deposit the blue egg inside before the next one comes soaring across the room. With the folded towel clenched in her fingers, she dives again, tumbles in a perfect 'o', and opens her hands to find the white egg intact. This one's a goose egg, and larger. She plops it in the box and readies herself at the mouth of the wall pocket once more.

Have you ever played goalie in football? Is it hard to catch the ball before it ploughs into the back of the net? Well, imagine if you were playing the game on dusty, foot-sliding rock. And imagine the back of the net was in fact the edge of a cliff. And imagine the football was tiny, and there were half a dozen of them, fired one after the other … and imagine they were eggs.

Tabitha Plimtock is the greatest goalie the world has ever known. Or at least she would be, if the world had any idea she exists. She leaps and dives and twists mid-air, catching all six eggs without cracking so much as a single shell.

'Get 'em all, did you, Tabby girl?' Mr Offal wipes sweat from his brow as he stands, smearing a trail of damp feathers over his eyes like an oddly shaped unibrow.

'Yes, Mr Offal,' Tabitha replies as she zips up her bag.

'Smashing, smashing. Then come and have a sit down and I'll fetch us something cool to drink.'

Tabitha's heart is still thumping as she sits in a threadbare armchair to one side of the wall pocket. There's a narrow bookcase behind her, with two rows of books, and a small coffee table that was once an upturned crate, where Mr Offal puts the tray. Tabitha watches dismally as he pours her a glass but smiles as he hands it to her. It's orange in colour, but it isn't juice. Duck and goose eggs are pretty much all that Mr Offal knows or has, and so the gloopy liquid swilling around in her glass is actually beaten eggs. But the man is always kind, and Tabitha is nothing if not polite.

'Thanks, Mr Offal, you're very good.'

He drops into the chair opposite. 'It's nothing, my dear girl. You come so far, after all. Can't have you passing out from dehydration when you get back on that green monstrosity. How is the climbing today?'

'It's lovely. The sun is out and you can see almost all the way down to Mr Cratchley's.'

Mr Offal shudders. 'Wouldn't like that, my dear. The dark bit? Gives me the willies. I never look down. Never look up much neither. What's there to see?'

'Really?' says Tabitha. 'But there's so much to see. Blue sky, white clouds, birds flying around–'

'Got my birds here to look at.'

'Yes, of course, but these are other birds, different birds, and they fly so high.'

'Showing off, that's all that is. I don't need to look outside my door to see some fancy birds showing off. My birds are just fine, thank you very much.'

Tabitha is sorry she mentioned it.

'Of course they are,' she says, 'and they lay the most scrumptious eggs that make the very best cakes.'

'Do they?' Mr Offal is smiling now.

'Absolutely. I've brought you half a cherry and almond today.'

She pulls out a parcel wrapped in cloth and hands it over.

'That'll do nicely, Tabby girl. Slice of that with my tea later and I'll be a happy camper.'

'And I'm returning your book too. Thank you so very much, I don't think I've ever enjoyed a story more.'

'Ah,' Mr Offal says, taking the book and reading the spine, 'the one about tiny people, is it?'

Tabitha smirks, knowing full well he's playing with her.

'*Little Women*,' she replies, 'and you know they're regular-sized.'

'Aye,' he says, placing the book back on the shelf, 'that is a good one alright. Bawled my eyes out when … oh, did you get to that bit?'

'About Beth? Yes, I read the whole thing. I cried at that part too.' Tabitha sighs. 'But it must be lovely, in a way.'

'Lovely, Tabby girl? Whaddya mean? Broke my heart, that did.'

'Yes, but it broke her family's hearts too, because they loved her so much. And that's what's lovely – a family who love each other.'

'I guess that's true.'

'Do you have any family, Mr Offal?'

'Me? Had an uncle way back when. Taught me how to raise birds. Died a long time ago, mind.'

'And do you miss him?'

Mr Offal squints like he's gazing into the horizon. 'Don't know that I miss him, as such. I mean, I used to notice that he wasn't there. Is that the same thing? Don't notice anymore though, been so long. And he was a dreadful bore, if I remember rightly. Never spoke, except to the birds, and even then he used to put them to sleep.' He sniffs and wipes his nose. 'Drink up there, Tabby girl. Eggs are best when they're fresh. And grab yourself another book, if you want. Aren't too many to choose from, I know.'

When Tabitha is leaving Mr Offal's, the sky is beginning to darken. She looks up at strings of grey cloud creeping over the sun and frowns. If the rain starts pelting down over the cliff face, it will make the next part of her journey very dangerous indeed.

CHAPTER FOUR

THE WAILING TWINS

A storm is brewing. The net billows slowly in the growing wind, throwing eerie shadows over the rock. Tabitha shivers in her thin woollen jumper and wonders how the sky can get so dark in the middle of the day. She climbs lower, seeing the outline of the wailing twins' shack sticking out from the wall like a splintered wooden tick. The timber beams are rickety and they creak in the wind. She can already hear a low, swelling moan, as if a wounded wolf is trapped inside.

But there is no wolf. It is Merry Lost who wails.

She stands at the window overlooking the fall like a wispy ghost, long hair trailing out past the curtains. Her skinny fingers hold her face, pulling down on her cheeks so you can see the pink bit below her eyeballs, and her mouth is stretched wide.

'Ooooh,' she cries out to the grey clouds, 'ooooh, woe. Woe is me. Ooooooh.'

'Hello, Merry.' Tabitha steps off the net and onto the porch of the shack, very close to the long, forlorn face.

'Sweet child' – Merry snatches her wrist with one hand – 'look not into the abyss, for darkness grows in the heart of the sky.'

'Yes, the weather has taken a bit of a turn, hasn't it?'

Merry pulls her close so that Tabitha is pressed up against the windowsill. 'Beware the evil that lurks in the changing of the winds.'

'I'll try not to catch a chill, but I don't think it'll drop below freezing or anything. How's Jerry today?'

Merry's eyes stay wide. 'Come inside, child, and

shelter for a while. My brother lies prostrate.'

'He's what?' Tabitha says, then she notices Jerry Lost curled up on a bunk at the back of the room. 'Oh, he's having a nap, I see. Yes, I'll just pop in for a moment if you don't mind. Have a few things on the list.'

The wailing twins' shack (they're called the wailing twins because … well, you've seen some of the wailing already – they do that a lot) has windows on three sides and is somehow still dark inside. It's always cold too. There is a stove, but the twins never light it. Fire brings to life evil spirits that are hiding in the stove – Merry has seen them escaping through the grate. Tabitha has seen them too. The evil stove spirits looked and smelled very much like smoke.

Tabitha holds out a piece of paper. 'A few herbs and nuts, if you've got them to spare, and some more cinnamon. That stuff is just lovely. Bertha loves it in her cakes. I can pay you in bread today, and I can

spare a couple of eggs too, if you need them. Mr Offal's long-toed webbers do lay such big eggs.'

Merry peruses the list. 'Ah, rosemary. For protection, no?'

'More for stews and things.'

'Ah.'

For a mournful woman, Merry is surprisingly light on her feet. She crawls onto the window ledge on one side of the shack and plucks leaves from several bushes growing in a crate. She digs up a handful of peanuts from the soil, then crawls up a wooden beam, like a sad salamander, and scurries over the gutter and onto the roof. There is a gnarly tree growing just above the shack, and Merry gets the cinnamon from its bark.

Tabitha wanders around the shack as she waits, peering at the few slim volumes on a bookshelf (they all seem to be catalogues of ghosts and other supernatural creatures, or guides on how to avoid them) and at the labels on funny-shaped bottles.

Disappearing Potion – Handle With Care

Rot Blot – Avoid Direct Contact With Skin

The East Wind

The West Wind (note: some of the North Wind got in before bottle was sealed)

Jerry's Tooth

'Merry,' Tabitha says when the woman climbs back through the window, 'this Disappearing Potion, does it really work?'

'Ooooh!' Merry holds her hands up in horror. 'Do not touch, child! Yes, the potion is extremely potent.'

'Really?'

'Why, yes. It was less than one month ago when a lonely traveller made the grave error of underestimating its power.' Merry settles on the arm of a chair to tell the story. She gazes into the distance, as if that's where the memory lies. 'It was a day much like today, except it was night, when the wind was howling and the rain lashed against the window panes.'

Tabitha looks outside and sighs. It has indeed begun to rain heavily. Merry goes on.

'The spirits were stirring and there was an unsettled air in the … in the air. The moon shone bright through the crashing rain and all of a sudden, there was a knock at the door.'

Knock, knock.

Tabitha jumps. She looks around and can't tell where the sound came from – it was like an echo of a knock, still reverberating through the room. Merry doesn't seem to notice. She goes on.

'He wore a hood, his face covered, and asked in a deep, gravelly voice for a moment's shelter from the storm. Visitors here are few and far between, my dear child, so you can imagine our apprehension. But we allowed the man to come inside. He did not lower his hood but walked around mysteriously' – Merry's hands move as if following the visitor – 'and he plucked that very bottle from the dresser. I warned him; I told him it held a potion with the power to disappear a man, and he just laughed. Then he popped the cork and swallowed deeply. "Quite nice," the stranger said, "bit bitter." When I told him of the herbs we grow on the window, he crawled onto the sill to take a look. I turned my head for a second, no more, heard a sound like a foot sliding on floorboards, a little cry, and he was gone. Disappeared.'

'Oh dear,' Tabitha says, 'he fell?'

'*Disappeared*,' Merry says, as if Tabitha hasn't spoken, 'into thin air. We never saw him again.'

'Well, I guess not. I mean, it's a very long fall and–'

'*Spirits!*'

The shriek makes Tabitha drop the bottle, which smashes. Jerry Lost sits bolt upright on his bunk, his hands clawed in the air.

'Spirits,' he cries again, 'unsettle my sleep. Oooooh, oooooh, woe. Woe is me!'

'Hello, Jerry,' Tabitha says. 'Sorry about the bottle there, I got a fright.'

Jerry turns, his face screwed up in anguish. 'Hello, child.'

'Merry was just telling me the story about that man who visited last month, the one who fell from the windowsill.'

Jerry rushes to Tabitha's side and clasps her hand. 'An omen. An omen, child, of worse to come. They crawl up from the deep.'

'What is this, brother?' Merry clasps Tabitha's other hand and Tabitha is kind of stuck between them as they howl and wail at each other's words.

'I saw it in my dreams,' Jerry says. 'Something stirs, from deep in the dark.'

'From the dark?' says Merry.

'From the dark!'

'Oh, woe!'

'Woe, indeed!'

'Well, I'd better be off.' Tabitha squeezes her hands from all four of theirs. 'Have a few more things on the list to get. Lovely seeing you both.'

It's raining horribly, with streaks of lightning cracking the sky. Tabitha's heart sinks, but it's best she leaves now or she could get stuck for hours listening to the mournful wail of the twins. As she steps over the threshold, Jerry grabs her arm.

'Beware what crawls from the dark of the wall.' He gazes into the storm. 'The winds are changing, and no-one is safe.'

'Okey doke, Jerry. See you soon.'

Tabitha climbs onto the net as sharp hailstones spike through her thin jumper. The vines are wet and slippery and she has to watch her feet.

Chapter Five

AERIAL GOATS

Goats are remarkable creatures. It is a little-known fact that goats excel at the art of trapeze. Their dexterity and extraordinary sense of balance make them nature's aerialists. This fact is little known because so few goats have access to trapeze equipment, but their talent for climbing on a knife's edge and balancing on the tiniest of rocky outcrops is evident on every mountain range and coastal cliff these wonderful animals inhabit. I'm sure you've seen it – in pictures if not in real life – a goat, higher up a mountain than any awkward-looking four-legged animal has any right to be, standing perfectly still above a hundred-metre drop without a care in the world. We humans find it almost impossible to comprehend.

And that is because of the goat's great joke. A goat is no fool, but she will happily allow you to believe otherwise. A goat in a farmyard totters around on bandy legs, making awful honking noises and pretending to be stupid. With eyes set very far apart and flat ears flopping out to the sides like the wings of a droopy airplane, a goat will often add to her silly appearance by flaring her nostrils and letting her tongue hang out of her mouth. Children laugh at goats in farmyards. Adults do too.

'Look at that silly goat,' an adult will say to a toddler at their knee. 'Isn't that a silly goat?'

And the toddler will giggle and squeal in agreement, and the goat will let her tongue hang out even further.

But a goat is no fool. A goat has more poise and inner peace than the most yogic of yoga instructors. What you see in the farmyard is merely an act – a little bit of whimsy – for the goat's own amusement.

Tabitha Plimtock is one of those rare humans who doesn't dismiss the goat as a stupid, awkward creature. As a regular climber on the cliff wall, she knows what skill and courage is required to climb the way goats do. She understands that they are special, and she pays attention.

In case you forgot, Tabitha is currently descending the vine net in a hailstorm. Below and to her left there is a clump of dark brown huddled against the rock. The storm worsens and Tabitha heads towards the dark-brown thing, hoping to find shelter for a few minutes. The goat must have been waiting for her, for as soon as Tabitha is level with him and can look the animal in the eye, he uncrouches and begins moving to the left. Tabitha doesn't like leaving the safety of the net in such bad weather, and she can't hop and jump as delicately as the goat, but she follows anyway, putting her feet where his feet had been just seconds before. Very quickly they come to a small outcrop jutting out from the wall. The goat perches on top like a shaggy-haired buddha, taking deep breaths in the rain. Tabitha crawls onto the ledge beneath and is able to sit cross-legged, sheltered from the storm.

'Thank you,' she calls up to the goat.

He doesn't answer.

The rain eases after a while and the sun even starts to peek through the clouds.

'Hut, hut. Come on now. Hut, hut.'

There is someone moving towards Tabitha, walking perpendicular to the wall and waving a stick. It looks like he has jammed his feet into two very large, coloured raindrops, but the raindrop-looking things are squidgy and squashy and extremely sticky. With these squashy, sticky blobs of glue, he walks along the wall as if the wall were the ground, picking up his knees with each step – *schlopp*, *schlopp* – in order to pull the glue loose.

He's got drops of glue on his wrists too, for use in

climbing, but he's not using those right now. There's a goat hopping ahead of him, and he seems unable to coax her back. While swinging the stick and cursing the goat, he notices Tabitha tucked under the outcrop.

'Tabby, you little pet! What are you doing on the wall today? The weather's absolutely brutal.'

'Hi, Richard,' Tabitha says, crawling out from her spot in the rock. 'It is a bit miserable now, but it was sunny when I left. Besides, I have today's list to get through.'

'Those relatives of yours …' Richard sniffs. 'Well, if I can't say something nice, I suppose I'd better shut my trap. Find yourself a little cubbyhole there, did you?'

'The goat led me to it.'

'Did he, now?' Richard looks sceptical. 'Don't kid yourself, my little plum, these beasts are thick as two short planks.'

Tabitha climbs to sit atop the outcrop as the goat

hops away. 'I really think you underestimate them, you know. They're very smart.'

'Smart, my eye. I've been trying to milk this one for a bleedin' hour now, and …' He makes a swipe at the grey and white goat ahead of him. She pirouettes out of his way and bleats. 'See that? Twits.'

As Richard makes his way towards Tabitha, she can hear the *schlopp, schlopp* of the raindrop glue on his feet. He sits next to her on the rock and she asks, 'Where's Molly today?'

'Look out abooooove!'

The sudden cry from below gets louder and louder until a body zips past the outcrop and up into the air. Tabitha catches a glimpse of Molly's smiling face as the woman flies by.

'Hello, Molly!'

'Tabby, sweetheart' – the voice is far away as Molly slows to a stop in the air, high up the wall – 'what a sight you are for sore eyes.' The voice gets louder again when Molly plunges back down into another bungee dive past the outcrop. 'Out shopping, are you?'

'Yes, I–' Tabitha stops short as Molly's zooming past whips her hair into her face.

'For heaven's sake, Moll,' Richard calls to the disappearing figure below, 'pull over for a second, will you? How's the girl supposed to talk to you when you're flipping about like a moth in a lamp?'

'Right you are, my love,' comes the reply.

Molly begins to wind in the bungee string of glue attached to her waist. Her bounces get shorter and shorter until the string is wound all the way into the spot where it's stuck to the wall. Then, crouched like a beetle, she crawls up to meet the other two, rolls the glue string into an oblong shape, fixes it to the rock and sits on it.

'Sorry about that, sweetheart,' she says. 'Was collecting that phosphorescent algae stuff from down below the sunline.'

'Don't listen to that rubbish.' Richard nudges

Tabitha. 'It's all about the bungee. She lives for the thrill. And poor me, here, trying to get on and milk that lot all by myself.'

'The algae's a good earner, I'll have you know,' Molly says.

'Glow-in-the-dark moss? What's that good for?'

'Honestly, Rich, you've no imagination. Stick it in a jar and it's a nightlight,' she replies. 'I've been trading this stuff for weeks. The wailing twins love it. Got that mystical blue glow. They moaned for a good hour over the first one.'

Her husband rolls his eyes and tuts.

'Don't mind him,' Molly says to Tabitha, smiling. 'How've you been, love? Good day out so far?'

'Yes, not bad. The twins were especially waily today though. Jerry had a nightmare and kept going on about the dark, and something stirring. It set Merry off terribly.' Molly and Richard exchange meaningful looks, which Tabitha doesn't miss. 'What?'

'Well, pet,' Richard says, 'there might be something to that.'

CHAPTER SIX

THE WHATEVER-THEY-ARES

Richard shifts over to sit closer to Tabitha. The metal milk canisters on his back rattle like chains.

'There are rumours,' he says, 'of things lurking at the bottom of the wall.'

'What things?' says Tabitha.

'*Terrible* things.'

'Richard,' Molly says, 'don't be so dramatic.'

'I'm just telling it like it is, Molly, my love.'

His wife tuts. 'You'll scare the poor girl.'

'Is there something to be scared of?' asks Tabitha.

'Well ...' Molly takes Tabitha's hand like she's a teacher about to give her a failing grade. 'We've been hearing rumours on and off now that things are changing down below, down at the base of the wall.'

'Is there a base of the wall?'

'Yes, somewhere very far down – very, *very* far down – there's an end to it. Anyway, it used to be very cold and very damp at the base.'

'No sunlight ever reaches it, you see?' Richard says. 'So it never warms up.'

'Exactly,' says Molly, 'and whatever lives down there likes it that way. But lately it's been less cold.'

'The edge is getting warmer and dustier,' says Richard. 'It's making the weather weird – it gets too hot in summer, too stormy in winter, and in between it's ... well, it's weird.'

'The weather has been a bit unpredictable recently,' Tabitha agrees, thinking of all the times she's stepped onto the net in blistering sunshine and come home shivering, soaked to the skin.

'At the base the change is more extreme, and food is becoming scarce. So they're moving up.'

'They?' Tabitha shivers.

'The whatever-they-ares. They're moving up to search for food. And when they find it – CRUNCH!' Richard claps his hands together and grimaces.

'Stop scaring the girl!' Molly snaps.

'Oh, sorry,' Richard says, patting Tabitha's hand, 'but you've nothing to worry about, my plum. Your house is right at the top of the cliff. They'll have eaten all of us before they ever get to you.'

'They eat *people*?' Tabitha says.

'Who knows? Probably. It's impossible to say. No-one's actually seen one yet.'

'Then how do you know they exist?'

'Because animals are going missing.'

Tabitha frowns. 'I'm not sure I believe you.'

'We didn't believe it either, Tabby, sweetheart.

Until Blondie disappeared.'

'Your goat?'

'My favourite,' Richard sighs. 'I mean, as much as one can have a favourite goat. She was the one that annoyed me the least – always came when I called. But I called for her two weeks ago and she didn't come. Haven't seen her since.'

'Poor Blondie!'

'Mmm.'

'But no-one's disappeared above the sunline yet,' Molly says hurriedly, 'so you stay above the dark, pet, and you'll be fine.'

'But Mr Cratchley lives below the sunline,' Tabitha replies.

Climbing down into the dark where the sun can't reach is not Tabitha's favourite thing, but it's always worth it to see Mr Cratchley. She thinks of his little home, with all its wonderful treasures stacked on shelves, and the lovely smile they bring to his face, and she feels sad.

'Besides,' she says, suddenly determined, 'you drop into the dark all the time.'

'For a second or two at the most,' Molly says. 'That's why I'm on the glue string. I can snatch a handful of algae and pop back up to the real world before a whatever-they-are can possibly grab me. But climbing down? Tabby, love, I think it's best you go without seeing Cratchley.'

'For now at least,' Richard says, trying to soften the blow. 'Maybe sometime in the future things will change again. The base may go cold, the whatever-they-ares will stay down there, and everything will go back to the way it was.'

Molly takes her hand. 'Promise us you won't go down there anymore.'

They stare at her, both staying silent until they get an answer.

'Alright,' Tabitha says at last.

'Well, that's all sorted then,' says Richard. 'So, what'll it be today, my little flower? Half a pound of butter and a can of milk?'

Tabitha smiles, nods and pays for the butter and milk. When Richard wanders off in search of his goats, and Molly resumes her algae hunt, Tabitha gazes down the wall. Far below, the rock descends into darkness. She wonders if she can see something moving down there – something big, with sharp teeth and tentacles. Maybe the whatever-they-ares are hairy, maybe they're bald. Maybe they swallow people whole, or maybe they spit on them to digest them first, then suck them up, like flies.

Animals are going missing.

Tabitha wonders if anyone has checked if Mr Cratchley is missing.

***

The sun is beginning to set as Tabitha works her way back to the net. She's running a little late – Gower and Gristle and Cousin Wilbur will be tapping their feet impatiently, waiting for her to make the dinner. Tabitha usually makes the dinner. The only time she gets a break is when Gower is on another health kick; then he makes a kidney bean bake, or some other foul recipe he's just come up with.

She glances down to the dark one more time. She doesn't have time to descend all the way down there now and, after her promise to Molly and Richard, Tabitha would feel very guilty betraying them right away. But she does mean to break her promise at some point. She can't imagine going the rest of for-ever without seeing Mr Cratchley.

As she begins her ascent back to the house, she thinks of the first time she met Mr Cratchley. She had been very young, only five or six years old, but already a master climber. The Plimtocks had been sending her down the net since the first day she learned to walk. Exploring the nooks and crannies of the wall, she had met Mr Offal, the wailing twins, Molly and Richard and the goats. She learned to love the wall –

it was the place where she was happy, where all these wonderful people lived, and where she could be away from the house at the top of the cliff. But being an inquisitive five- or six-year-old, she wondered what lay in the dark further down the wall, where the sunlight couldn't reach.

'Never go below the sunline,' people had told her. 'There's nothing down there but darkness.'

But there had to be more than that, Tabitha had been sure of it. If there was more wall, there were more wall pockets. If there were more wall pockets then surely someone, or something, lived in them.

It was a rainy Wednesday the first day she went down there. The grey clouds darkened the wall, which made the blackness below seem a little less foreboding. Little Tabitha climbed lower and lower on the vine net. The air got colder. The rock felt colder too, and damp under her fingertips. In those days she climbed barefoot, no matter the weather; her feet were growing too quickly, and Gower refused to trade for any more shoes until 'those wretched feet of yours stop growing, you little snot'.

Tabitha had stopped just above the sunline and waited there for several minutes. It was ever so gloomy looking down. There were different smells than she was used to, wafting up from the shadows. It was scary gazing down into the unknown.

But Tabitha refused to be afraid. There were monsters in the world – dangerous animals and mean people – but there were also beautiful flowers and kind friends, and goats and raindrops and sweet smells and love. If you gaze into the unknown and only ever see monsters, then surely you'll miss out on all the wonderful things hidden therein.

Little Tabitha smiled to herself, then slid off the bottom of the net and climbed down into the darkness.

CHAPTER SEVEN

MR CRATCHLEY

The cold had been enough to make her teeth chatter. She looked around as she descended, but once the sunlight was gone there was nothing to see; nothing that her eyes could see anyway. The wind whispered and whistled and sounded different. It sounded on purpose, like the wind was a person who liked their own voice. It whistled high and whispered low, and little Tabitha had felt it was playing for her. She didn't know if that made her happy or made her nervous.

She had continued down the clammy rock until something tickled her finger. Surprised, she lifted that hand and felt more tickling on the other.

Tabitha traced her fingertips over the stone and felt, too late, the tell-tale burrows and squiggly bodies of rock worms.

'Oh no!' she cried before the rock crumbled under her hands and she went plummeting down.

SNAP. With the sound, she felt something clamp around her ankle. She was dangling upside down in the dark, her arms and other leg hanging freely in the cold, damp air. Little Tabitha was too young at that time to have had any experience of death, and yet her sharp mind wondered if she had passed over to the other side. She had no memory of hitting the ground, but maybe your brain covered that up to save you the pain.

There was a snuffle. The sniffing sound of someone about to sneeze.

'Hello?' Tabitha said.

'*Atchooooo!*'

Like something on a spring, Tabitha was vaulted up and backwards, landing on her bottom on soft carpet.

She marvelled at what she saw around her. Glowing lines of blue stretched like a friendly web, from the ground in front of her all the way up the walls and across the ceiling. To her right was the same, but these lines were pink. She turned to look behind, where a tangle of pale-green luminescence wound up and around the rock. The three pulsing colours met in the centre of the roof and curled around each other, like shapes in a kaleidoscope.

'It's beautiful,' she had breathed, quite overcome.

'Thank you.'

Little Tabitha had almost forgotten that someone had snatched her ankle and thrown her into this place. An old man stood in the doorway of the wall pocket, almost invisible against the dark outside.

'Did you catch me?' she asked.

'I did.'

'Thank you.'

'You're very welcome.'

There was a long silence and Tabitha wondered if

this stranger had ever had visitors before.

'My name is Tabitha.'

'Hello, Tabitha. It's nice to meet you.'

The stranger stood still in the dark and said no more until she prompted him.

'What is your name?'

'My name is Bob Cratchley.'

'It's nice to meet you, Mr Cratchley. I didn't know anyone lived down here in the ... down below the sunline.'

He didn't seem to know how to respond to that, and he went silent again. Tabitha stood up, enjoying the soft, fluffy feeling of the moss carpet between her bare toes, and wandered around the wall pocket. This made Mr Cratchley anxious; he seemed to go tense. He reached out one hand, but then pulled it back and Tabitha took that as permission to have a look around his place. She was curious, and dying to see how someone lived in a pocket below the sunline.

The wonderfully coloured web on the walls was

luminescent algae, several species that were not only different in colour, but also in shape. The blue was blobby, the pink stringy and the green had lovely spiral strands.

'It's like a garden,' Tabitha said.

'Yes,' Mr Cratchley replied. 'I take good care of it.'

There were shelves dotted all over the pocket – short ones, long ones, stacked ones, curved ones – all tucked into the gaps of the glowing web. There were objects on each shelf, some of them familiar, some of them very strange. A paper airplane perched on one; it was very old, the paper yellowed and crinkly around the edges like it had been caught in the rain. There was a spectacular feather from what must have been a gigantic bird. It was nearly a metre long and had shimmering eyes of blue and green all along the length of it.

'Wow,' said Tabitha.

She reached out to touch it and heard a sharp intake of breath. She turned and jumped. Mr Cratchley had silently migrated from his spot by the door and was standing very close, his hands tightly clenched together.

'I won't touch anything,' Tabitha said. 'I'll just look.'

'Okay,' he replied, but he seemed very worried.

He was a thin man and dreadfully pale, and Tabitha wondered if he missed the sunshine. Maybe he had never even seen it before. The skin sagged from his cheekbones as if it was tired, and his eyes bulged and watered and were quite red. Mr Cratchley looked like a man who had been crying for years and years.

He followed closely as Tabitha moved about the wall pocket, and she was careful not to touch the items on the shelves lest he get upset. It took a lot of self-control, however; she was not used to seeing such beautiful things. Gristle often returned from scavenging trips with stuff that she had found or bartered for with travellers, but much of it was junk – broken household appliances rusted and filled with dust from the edge, or smelly old shoes with holes in the soles. Most of Gristle's finds were dumped in a growing pile on one side of the house. The objects on Mr Cratchley's shelves were not like that. There was a bright-red scarf so delicate and soft in appearance that Tabitha was desperate to feel the material. She clasped her hands together and knelt down to view the shelves underneath. There was an earring with several silver fish hanging from it, all hammered wafer thin. There was a small cardboard box with shiny gold trim and purple swirls all over it. Below that was a letter; the writing was joined and difficult to read, but Tabitha could make out the closing words: *Love always, Alanna xx.*

'These are lovely things,' Tabitha whispered.

'Thank you.'

'But where do they come from?'

'The wind brings them.'

She looked up at him, confused, and he scuttled to the doorway and pointed. It was so dark outside that even at the edge of the rock Tabitha could see only blackness. Mr Cratchley took a firm hold of her wrist.

'Lean out,' he said, 'but keep your feet on the threshold.'

She did so, trusting him not to drop her; for such a wiry man, he was very strong.

The air was cold and so damp on her skin it was almost as if there was a constant spray of tiny, tiny droplets in the atmosphere. As she hung in the black her eyes adjusted to the dark and she could make out shapes. On either side of the wall pocket hung long, wavy strips. She reached out and touched the edge of one; it felt leathery and cold, but also a little sticky. She tapped a finger on the flat of it and it stuck fast.

'Oh no,' she said.

The leathery strip flapped back and forth as she tried to pull her finger free.

'Wiggle your hand gently from side to side,' came Mr Cratchley's voice from above, 'and it will let go.'

He was right. Tabitha's finger came unstuck.

'Thanks,' she said. 'I'm ready to come up now.' He tugged her back inside the wall pocket. 'What are those sticky things?'

'Rockweed,' he replied. 'It helps me to collect things. It catches what the storms bring in, grabs them right out of the air.'

'But where do the things come from?'

'From the world.'

Tabitha knew a little about the world – she learned about it in books that Mr Offal was teaching her to read, and sometimes she met travellers when she walked in the woods near the edge – but it still seemed a place so far away.

'From where in the world?'

'From everywhere.'

It was then that Tabitha noticed an orange glow at the back of the wall pocket. On a very high shelf, on which it stood alone, was a large jar with a heart drawn on it. Inside was the most wonderful sight – tiny drops of light, hundreds of them, whizzing around and bouncing off the glass. She had never seen anything more beautiful.

'What is that?' she asked, and for the first time Mr Cratchley smiled, a painful kind of smile.

'That's my jar of lost love.'

Tabitha reached out a finger to softly tap the glass and he didn't stop her.

'Lost love?'

'The people of the world are so very lucky,' he said, 'but they don't know it. They have so much love in their lives that they sometimes let it go. They give it away or forget about it, and it falls away from them and gets caught on the wind.'

'But that's so sad. Do the bits of love get stuck to the rockweed too?'

'Oh no, I catch those with my hands.' Mr Cratchley's eyes looked even more watery than before. 'And I keep them safe.'

Tabitha traced the flitting love-lights with her fingertips. 'If I had anything so wonderful, I'd never let it go.'

'Neither would I.'

CHAPTER EIGHT

LAUNDRY DAY

In case you've forgotten, Tabitha (that is, older Tabitha, as she is now) is climbing home after her shopping trip. She is thinking about the first time she met Mr Cratchley and wondering if he's okay; she also can't stop thinking about the whatever-they-ares and if they really exist.

Whether the horrors below are real or not, she knows that the horrors above most certainly are. The windows of the house at the edge of the cliff are all wide open. They are banging against the brickwork as if the house is flapping its hands and feet, desperate to get away from something horrible and rotten. But it can't, because what's horrible and rotten sits inside the house. It is Bertha's laundry day.

Tabitha counts up the days in her mind. It can't possibly be laundry day already – she's sure she had at least another week – but as she steps onto the sill of her bathroom window, the smell hits her like a massive, sweaty bat that's lost control and toppled out of the air straight into her face. It very nearly knocks her off the sill.

Bertha's laundry day requires some explanation. The woman rarely moves from her spot on the beanbag in the front room. The woman also eats a colossal amount of cake. Have you ever eaten a very large slice of birthday cake and then felt a little sick afterwards? Perhaps your tummy felt a bit hard and round, kind of like a bowling ball. The most likely explanation for that particular sensation is gas. Human gas. And it's perfectly normal. Everybody gets a little gassy from time to time, and it's usually relieved by a small expelling of said gas in one way or another.

Eating foods like birthday cake can bring on one of

these small bouts of gas, but what would happen if you spent an entire day eating birthday cake? How much gas would accumulate? The thought alone is probably making your tummy feel a little uncomfortable right now. Well, I'm about to make it worse. Imagine you ate nothing but birthday cake for an entire week. Now imagine it for an entire year. Now imagine it for an entire *lifetime*. The amount of gas collecting in your poor tummy would probably defy measurement. And, horrible though it would be, that gas would have nowhere to go but out. The seat on which you placed your bottom would be under constant assault. It would suffer unthinkable bombardment. That seat would be like a bullseye at a carnival shooting gallery, with nothing but sharp-shooters lining up to play. It would be like a bird, trapped in the churning winds of a never-ending smelly cyclone. That seat would be tormented by gas.

Bertha's beanbag is that seat. She perches on her spot from dawn until dusk, farting away, filling that poor unfortunate beanbag with putrid, foul-smelling vapour. And while the woman remains perched on her spot, her bottom shields the world from the worst of the horrors festering underneath. It acts as a barrier to the stench, a tweed-covered roadblock that keeps its rotten traffic trapped within the confines of the beanbag. But when Bertha moves, when she senses that the bag is filled to capacity, she declares a laundry day. And that is when the road-block is removed.

Bertha rolls off her beanbag and the poor, put-upon bag cries out for help. Air escapes from between the tiny beans and rushes forth, bringing with it everything that Bertha has been forcing in since the last laundry day. It is dreadful. Odour fills the house and there is nowhere to hide: you can duck behind the curtains, but the smell will find you; you can dive under the bed, but the smell will find you; you can pinch your nose with your fingertips until it hurts, and still the smell will find a way to burrow in between the clenched edges of your nostrils. There is no escape.

Tabitha teeters on the bathroom windowsill, knowing that Gower, Gristle and Cousin Wilbur have already done what they always do – thrown the windows open in panic and then fled the house. They won't be in the garden – that's too close to ground zero – and they won't be by the pond, which is not far enough either. They might have gone all the way to the rock wood or the Lonely Tavern to avoid the stench. Wherever they've gone, they won't be back until the beanbag is laundered and dinner is on the table.

Tabitha dons a clothes peg on her nose – though that only helps a little – and fills the metal tub in the garden with water and enough soap to make the bubbles spill over the sides. In the front room she grabs the offending bag on one side and drags it out the door. Bertha, sitting in a temporary chair in the corner, is moaning already.

'Be quick about it,' she says. 'This chair is giving me splinters. You'll have to fish them out, you know, before I can sit back on the beanbag. The longer it takes, the more splinters you'll have to pull. So think about that.'

Tabitha does, and she heaves the fart-filled bag into the metal tub as quickly as she can. Feeling faint from the fumes, she digs at it with a long lump of timber, turning it over and swishing it about. She keeps swishing until her arms and back are too sore to swish anymore, then she pulls the bag out of the water (with a lot of effort – a soaked beanbag is about twenty times heavier than a dry one) and throws it over the thick washing line. It still smells bad, but after all the water has dripped out and the wind has blown at it for a few hours, it should smell tolerable enough to be returned to the front room.

The one good thing about beanbag laundry day is that Tabitha has some time to herself for a change. The others have escaped the house, so there's no-one around to boss her about, to tell her to do the dusting or clean the floors. She can take a few minutes to enjoy the peace and quiet.

Turning her back on Gristle's mountain of junk at one side of the house, she sits cross-legged at the edge of the pond and watches the sun set. There's a lovely orangey glow. It reminds her of Mr Cratchley's jar of lost love. She thinks of all those people out there in the world, so drunk on so much love that they can afford to lose it.

Something tickles her toes and she jumps. It's a newt that has crawled from the pond. It has a dark-red back and a purple belly, and very pale eyes.

'Hello,' says Tabitha.

The newt wriggles up her ankle, then scurries back down and into the water. There are more newts in there, dozens of them. Tabitha has never seen so many in the pond before. Some are red and purple, others are blue and green, some have spots and others have stripes. Tabitha watches them swimming around for a while, then heads back to the house. It's nearly sundown; Gower, Gristle and Cousin Wilbur will be wanting their dinner.

CHAPTER NINE

CURIOUS NEWTS

'Is there butter in this? There'd better not be butter in this, you little snot.' Gower is holding a spoonful of stew to his nose and sniffing in disgust. 'I power walked for two hours today, *and* did ninety minutes of high-kick aerobics, so you'd better not be undoing all my hard work. Is there butter in it?'

'There's no butter in it,' Tabitha says, slyly pushing the butter dish out of sight behind the bread bin.

There's about half a pound of butter in the stew, but Tabitha had to add that to make it edible. Gower has so many restrictions on what should and should not be on the dinner plate that she has to cheat a little. Besides, if she followed Gower's rules to the letter,

Gristle and Cousin Wilbur would spit the food back at her.

The wind has changed and Cousin Wilbur is currently an anteater. He sits at the table between Gower and Gristle, sucking up stew through the long protrusion on his face.

'Use a spoon, you rotten-faced rodent,' Gristle sniffs.

'An anteater's not a rodent, you dim-witted cow pat,' Cousin Wilbur replies, 'and I'll eat however I like.'

Tabitha sits on the counter – she is never offered a seat at the table, and she wouldn't want to sit there anyway. She doesn't usually speak during dinner, but she's curious to know if the rumours have made it to the top of the wall.

'I heard something interesting today,' she says.

Nobody asks what.

'It was about the weather and the wall and strange things coming up from the dark.'

There's no reply but chewing and the slurping of an anteater's snout.

'They say the strange things might eat people. People are nervous on the wall.'

Still no reaction, so Tabitha sits and eats her stew. Some minutes later Gower speaks.

'This stew is disgusting.' He has licked his bowl clean. 'And for the record, little snot, we don't like to hear about those degenerate insects living on the wall. And if something is coming to munch them up, what do we care?'

'What if the whatever-they-ares reach the top of the wall?' Tabitha says.

'There's no such thing as whatever-they-ares, you festering pusbag,' Cousin Wilbur snaps, 'and even if there was, we'd have nothing to do with them. That's the wall's problem.'

At that moment Tabitha kind of hopes the whatever-they-ares *are* real, and that they make it to the top of the wall, and that they gobble up the rotten inhabitants of the house at the edge of the cliff.

'Where's my beanbag?' Bertha shrieks from the

front room. 'Why do you all leave me with nothing to sit on but splinters?'

'Go bring it in,' Gristle says, tossing her dirty plate at Tabitha, 'and then do the dishes. I'm off to take a bath.'

Tabitha frowns. Gristle spends her days scavenging along the dusty edge and through the rock wood. She crawls into muddy holes and digs in soggy stream beds, and arrives home each evening covered from head to toe in muck. As a result, she always leaves the bath in a filthy state, and Tabitha will have to scrub the grime off the sides before she can lie down to sleep in it tonight.

Outside the evening air is chilled. Tabitha takes the beanbag off the line and is about to go inside when she notices a few dark shapes on the fence. They're standing to attention, and at first she thinks they are meerkats – Cousin Wilbur has been a meerkat on occasion – but a closer look shows some of them to have glow-in-the-dark spots or stripes on their backs. They're newts. And they're not just on the fence, they're on the ground outside the garden, they're all around the pond. There are more of them than she saw earlier. They're all watching her.

'You'd better not get caught in the garden,' Tabitha tells them. 'Gower and Gristle hate newts. Cousin Wilbur doesn't like them either, and if he's a cat or something bigger he'll chase you off or maybe even eat you.'

The newts don't look worried. They stand like little soldiers watching Tabitha as she hauls the slightly-less-foul-smelling beanbag indoors. When the door shuts and she's out of sight, the newts scurry off the fence and back to the pond.

* * *

Morning comes and the sun shines through the bath-room window. Tabitha unrolls her jumper-pillow and pulls on her jumper-jumper. It's Wednesday, Gristle's turn to bake a cake, which means Tabitha will have to drag her out of bed before her usual rising time of midday. It's always unpleasant. Gristle is a biter.

'You little wretch,' she growls as Tabitha pulls on one foot, 'you catastrophic windbag. You putrid, poo-filled puddle of goo. You rancid, blistering, bursting boil.'

'Good morning, Gristle.'

In the mounds of musty-smelling clothes on the floor, Tabitha finds trousers, a t-shirt and a pair of underpants that I would do better not to describe to you.

The wind must be blowing from east to west, because Cousin Wilbur looks like Cousin Wilbur. As Tabitha guides the still half-asleep and swearing Gristle into the kitchen, Cousin Wilbur glares at her.

'Tabitha, go get some cider.'

'Is the jug empty already? But I only went to the Lonely Tavern on Monday.'

Tabitha doesn't want to go. She's in a hurry to get her chores done and finish the day's shopping on the wall in time to pay a visit to Mr Cratchley.

'Are you calling me a liar?' Cousin Wilbur takes the empty jug from the fridge. 'Are you saying this jug is full? You sewage-spewing dung beetle! Perhaps you need to get squashed.'

Of all the Plimtocks, Cousin Wilbur has the foulest temper, and Tabitha knows he'll take any excuse to lose it.

'No, Cousin Wilbur, I'm not saying that at all. Yes, I can see the jug is empty. I'll go to the tavern now.'

With Tabitha compliant, Cousin Wilbur no longer has reason to scream blue murder. Disappointed, he hands Tabitha the heavy glass jug, making sure he clips Gristle on the side of the head while she sits, asleep, at the table.

'Ow!' Gristle jolts awake, grabs the can of milk in front of her and throws it.

Tabitha is too quick and it hits the wall.

'Now there'll be no milk for my bedtime cereal tonight!' Gristle whines.

'Tabitha,' Cousin Wilbur says, smiling, 'after you get the cider, go get some milk.'

* * *

As you might have guessed from the name, the Lonely Tavern is a rather empty place. The sign above the door actually says 'Lovely Tavern', but everyone calls it the Lonely Tavern, in part because it only ever has one or two customers sitting at its wood-wormed tables, and in part because the steady flow of tumbleweeds across the floor makes it look like the lonesomest place on Earth.

The tavern lies at the base of a ravine, between two great big dusty mountains. There are two large round holes in the walls that face each mountain, giving the tumbleweeds a clear path through the building. The story goes that a giant boulder once rolled from the top of one mountain into the ravine, crashing through the middle of the tavern and rolling up the mountain on the other side. The landlord grabbed some planks to fix the holes, but of course the boulder had reached the top of the second mountain and was rolling back down. It crashed through the few nailed-on planks and up the first mountain; once it reached the top it rolled back down again, and so on and so forth. The landlord and his customers learned to live with the ever-moving boulder, keeping the tables and the bar out of its path.

That was many, many years ago and the boulder is no longer rolling (nobody knows where it eventually ended up, perhaps it rolled off one side of a mountain and smashed into smithereens), but the holes in the walls are still there, and the much gentler tumbleweeds now use it to cross the ravine. To people like you and me, who have seen movies about the Wild West in America, that's what it would look like; a sandy, dusty saloon with rolling tumbleweeds. We'd expect the customers to be wearing cowboy hats and have their feet rattle with spurs when they walk, but the few customers the tavern has are nothing like that.

Tabitha, for instance, is one of them, and when she arrives at the place and plants the heavy glass jug on the bar, the landlady peers over at her with one single eye. The woman has an eye patch, you see – like a pirate – but that's a story for another day.

CHAPTER TEN

IN THE LONELY TAVERN

'Want me ter fill 'er up, lass?' says the landlady.

'Yes, please,' says Tabitha, 'and could you put it on our tab? I'll bring eggs next week.'

'Aye, that'll do grand.'

The landlady always speaks with a piratey growl. Tabitha's not sure if it's natural or if it's meant to complement the eye patch.

The woman lifts a huge wooden keg from the floor and balances it on her shoulder. Then she opens the tap and lets the fizzy golden liquid splash into the jug on the bar.

'How's the wall then?'

'Fine,' says Tabitha, 'I think.'

'Yer not sure?'

'Well, there are rumours about strange creatures crawling up the wall to munch on animals, and maybe people too.'

'Are there now?' says the landlady.

'Because of the change in the weather, someone told me.'

'Aye, that'd be right. Weather's been doing odd things as of late. Mountains been groaning too.'

'What do you mean?' Tabitha asks.

'Them mountains' – the landlady tips her head left and right – 'either side. They been groaning at nighttimes. Right racket they're makin'. Very unhappy about somethin', you mark my words. That it, lass?'

Tabitha nods and the landlady grasps the full jug with one hand and lowers it gently into Tabitha's arms.

'Sure you can manage that, lass? Right heavy for a

little rabbit like yerself. D'yer wanna hand?'

But years of daily climbing have made Tabitha's skinny arms far stronger than they look. She smiles and shakes her head.

'Suit yerself,' says the landlady. 'See yer soon, rabbit.'

Tabitha cradles the jug, careful not to spill a single drop, but nearly drops the entire thing when a customer grabs her shoulder before she reaches the door.

'Did you say things are crawling up the wall?'

The old man's eyes look wild and slightly vacant.

'That's what I've heard,' Tabitha replies.

'Up the wall? Munching on people, like crackers, you say?'

'Well, I didn't say it quite like that. Let go of my shoulder, please, you'll make me spill the cider.'

'Oi,' the landlady snaps from the behind the bar, 'you leave the rabbit be, Charlie, and get back ter yer table. Else I'll chuck you out the boulder hole.'

The man shudders under the threat and hurries back to his table. But behind his hand he whispers loudly to Tabitha, 'Find the doctor! You'll need the doctor, and you'll have to hurry. Please hurry, there's no time to lose!'

Tabitha leaves the tavern, stepping into the quiet sweetness of the rock wood, and wonders what he could possibly have meant.

The rock wood is a lovely place; a strip of forest that runs through the ravine. It's as green as anywhere gets at the edge of the world and is split fifty-fifty, half trees, half rocks. Tabitha crawls and climbs over the stones and boulders littered amongst the tree trunks, never once losing her grip on the jug in her hands. There's a little stream that runs down the middle of the wood, and she loves to take her shoes off and walk in it for as far as she can. The chill, clear water feels delightful on her bare feet.

She bends down to scoop a handful of water to her mouth and notices a familiar creature staring up at her. It sits with its purple belly resting on a stone and watches with its pale eyes. Now that Tabitha has seen one, like mushrooms in a field, she starts to see the others. They're swimming in the stream or lazing on damp rocks or scuttling under leaves, but they all appear to glance at her from time to time.

'Goodness,' Tabitha says, 'you lot are multiplying. You'll have taken over the whole edge soon.'

That makes her smile. She pictures Gower and Gristle perched on the upturned tub in the front garden, squealing and waving off hordes of newts. Cousin Wilbur could be dangling from the gable of the roof – as a blobfish or a naked mole rat – hissing and spitting at the ground. Bertha might be standing at the window, hollering that the newts have eaten all her birthday cake.

The rock wood seems suddenly brighter and even more pleasant than before, and Tabitha smiles.

'Hope you all have a wonderful day,' she says to the newts, then walks on, splashing her feet in the clear, cool stream.

* * *

Tabitha edges her way along the hundred-metre ledge to Mr Offal's wall pocket. She stuffs the rolled-up towel from the side of her backpack under her arm, ready to catch the first egg as she reaches the opening.

'Hello, Mr Offal. It's me, Tabitha.'

She steps onto the threshold and holds up the towel. But there is no egg. The place is silent.

'Mr Offal?'

Her heart sinks with dread until she sees a hunched shape sitting by the pen. Mr Offal sniffs and holds up a feather.

'My long-toed webber, Tabby girl. Little Fifi. Gone.'

'Gone? Gone where, Mr Offal?'

'It came in the night. Fierce big thing, but I didn't get a good look at it. It was like a shadow. Teeth like knives, though, I saw that much.'

'Oh, Mr Offal, I'm so sorry.'

He turns the big white feather in his fingertips and wipes his eyes with a handkerchief.

'My long-toed webber.'

Some time later Mr Offal has pulled himself together enough to sit with Tabitha in the pair of armchairs.

'There's no eggs for you today, my dear, I'm afraid,' he says. 'Birds left wouldn't lay.'

'Of course, Mr Offal, please don't worry about that.'

Tabitha can't help worrying about it herself though. She wonders what sort of cakes she can make without eggs, and wonders how many of them Bertha is likely to spit back out.

'Don't know if they'll ever lay again,' Mr Offal goes on. 'They were shaking something terrible afterwards. In my own home, can you imagine, Tabby girl? Cold-blooded murder in my own home. I've never seen the like. It's like something out of a horror novel.'

The mention of novels brings Tabitha's gaze to the bookshelf. She notices a volume there that she has not read. She has seen the book before, but never picked it up because the title didn't appeal: *Categorisation of Rock Worms and Other Edge Fauna*. But what she hadn't noticed before was the name of the author: Dr Wendy Sherback. *Doctor*.

'Mr Offal,' she says, 'where did you get that book from?'

'Which, Tabby dear? Oh, that one. One of my uncle's, that. He had an interest in that sort of thing, rock worms and wriggly things and the like. Was very proud of that particular book – signed copy, you know.'

'Signed copy,' says Tabitha. 'You mean he met the author?'

'Oh, she was a local, Dr Sherback. Well, she became a local after many years. Came from some university to study the wall, got obsessed with it and never left. She did expeditions to try and reach the base. Never managed it, as far as I know.'

'Do you know where she is now?'

'Sherback? Pfff, long gone probably. She was before my time – was around when my uncle was a young whippersnapper. If she's still alive she'd be about a million by now.'

* * *

'Doctor who?'

'Dr Sherback. Wendy Sherback.'

Tabitha has finally tracked down Richard as he follows his goat herd over the wall.

'Never heard of her,' he says. 'Molly, love, Dr Sherback, ring any bells?'

'Sherback?' Molly's voice drifts in and out as she flies up and down on a glue string. 'Nope, no bells ringing. Though my old gran used to talk about a creepy doctor who lived down the wall. Like, *way* down. But she'd be a million by now.'

'Tabby, sweetheart,' Richard says, 'if you're sick, the twins can knock up some pretty good home remedies.'

'No, no,' Tabitha says, 'she wasn't that kind of doctor. She studied insects and things. She wrote this, look.'

Tabitha shows him the book she has borrowed from Mr Offal and Richard nods, though he doesn't seem very enthusiastic.

'Well, that looks really old, which means she'd be really old, which means she's probably long gone.'

Tabitha puts the book away. 'Maybe.'

CHAPTER ELEVEN

BELOW THE SUNLINE

Tabitha hangs on the bottom of the vine net, looking down. Descending below the sunline is always a bit nerve-wracking, but now it's positively scary. The sun is close to setting so she's short on time, but Tabitha is determined to check on Mr Cratchley. Taking a deep breath she climbs off the net and down into the dark.

The kaleidoscope colours of his wall pocket are beautiful as always and, at the back, basking in the light of his lost love, stands Mr Cratchley. He turns at the sound of her entering and smiles.

'Hello, Tabitha.'

'Hello, Mr Cratchley.'

She is so relieved to see him alive and well that she feels the urge to rush forward and give him a hug. But hugs – and even handshakes – make him very uncomfortable, so she just smiles back instead.

'Caught some more last night,' he says, pointing to the jar.

'I thought it looked a little brighter.'

Without asking, he fills a cup with water from a trickle that runs down the back of the pocket and hands it to her. Then he takes something from a shelf and hands that to her as well. It's a blue ribbon.

'This came in on yesterday's winds. It's for you.'

'It's beautiful,' says Tabitha, 'but it's part of your collection and I know how important your things are to you. Doesn't it bother you to lose one?'

'It does.'

Tabitha holds out the ribbon, but the man shakes his head.

'I do find it difficult to give it away,' he says, 'but I also feel happy to have something to give you. So I've decided that this one is for you.'

He wraps it around her wrist and ties it in a bow.

'Thank you, I'll keep it safe.' There's a tear in Tabitha's eye. 'I'm so glad you're alright, Mr Cratchley.'

'Why wouldn't I be?'

She tells him about the rumours and the whatever-they-ares and the missing long-toed webber and the goat.

'So you see it's very dangerous at the edge right now, and I think you should move up the wall.'

'But the long-toed webber disappeared above the sunline.'

'Well, yes,' Tabitha says, 'but the whatever-they-ares are coming from the base, and I don't like the idea of you being alone down here.'

He smiles his painful, bulgy-eyed smile. 'You're very kind to care.'

'So you'll move up?'

'Oh no, I couldn't do that.'

He is still smiling and she knows there is no way to change his mind. He clasps his thin, frail hands in front of him and Tabitha feels a wave of worry. If a shadowy creature with knives for teeth were to ambush his home, he wouldn't stand a chance.

When Tabitha leaves she spends a few moments staring down into the dark below Mr Cratchley's wall pocket. She wonders if there really is a creepy doctor living down there. How far down might she be?

Tabitha should be back in the house on the edge of the cliff by now, but worry for Mr Cratchley gets the better of her and she starts to climb down. The air gets even colder. Soon it's frigid and her arms pimple with gooseflesh under her jumper. It's getting very damp too. Beads of cold water collect on her forehead and dribble down her cheeks. The wind howls and whispers and plays with her hair. There are sounds like things creeping and things crawling and things sharpening razor-edged teeth. Tabitha gulps.

She has been climbing for ages and she can't go any further. The lower down the wall she gets, the damper and slippier the rock gets. She can barely hold on, and if she keeps going she'll definitely fall. But as she turns back she sees something below – far, far, below: a fuzzy spot of pale light. From so far away it looks like one of Mr Cratchley's bits of lost love. There is something down there. Or someone.

The wind changes, blowing weeds on the rock that make dark shapes in the air. Tabitha takes one last look at the light she can never reach and starts climbing back up.

* * *

'You mucus-smothered waste of space.' The wind has changed again and Cousin Wilbur is a sour-faced iguana. 'You selfish, careless brat. Do you know how long we've been waiting for dinner?'

'I'm starving,' Gristle growls.

'And we're out of eggs for tomorrow's cake,' says Gower.

All three of them stand in the kitchen glaring at Tabitha.

'There were no eggs today,' Tabitha says. 'Mr Offal's birds were attacked last night, one of them was eaten and the others–'

'We don't want to hear your excuses, you little snot,' Gower snaps. 'How the hell are we supposed to make a cake without eggs?'

'I'll think of something,' she replies.

'Did you at least get milk?' Gristle says. 'If I have to go without my bedtime cereal tonight you're in for a bruising, you loser.'

Since Gristle was the one who threw the milk in the first place, Tabitha doesn't feel sorry for her.

'I did get milk.'

'And on top of it all,' Cousin Wilbur says, 'we've had to listen to Bertha screaming all day for a glass of cider. We've had to listen to her *all day* because you

weren't here to give her some.'

'You could have given her some yourself,' Tabitha replies. 'There's a full jug in the fridge.'

'Don't you talk back to me, you ugly little squirt.' Cousin Wilbur scurries over the counter so fast he makes her jump. 'Just you shut your lip and get on with the dinner.'

Tabitha doesn't argue. There's no point. Instead she puts a pot of water on the cooker to boil and fills a glass of cider.

Bertha's in a foul mood. She has screamed herself hoarse and is red in the face.

'Where the bloody hell have you been?' she says, snatching the glass and downing the cider in one long gulp.

Since the woman has a terrible memory, and Tabitha's in a pretty bad mood herself, the girl tells her exactly where she's been.

'I climbed down the wall as far as I could looking for Dr Wendy Sherback. I didn't see her today, but if she's still alive, and if there's any way she can help save the people on the wall from being munched up by monsters, then I intend to find her.'

Feeling a little better, Tabitha marches from the room but stops in the doorway when she hears Bertha say,

'Creepy Doctor Windy.'

CHAPTER TWELVE

THE GHOST IN THE ROCK WOOD

'What did you say?' Tabitha asks, coming back into the room.

'I want more cider!'

Tabitha quickly fetches her another glass and, after some pushing, Bertha starts to spill the beans.

'Always asking questions, the old bag,' she says, 'crawling round the garden fence with a magnifying glass. *Science*, she said. Pah! Waste of bloody time, science. What a dirty old windbag, Doctor Windy.'

A sour odour already seeping from Bertha's freshly laundered beanbag makes Tabitha want to say, 'That's the pot calling the kettle smelly', but she doesn't. Instead she asks, 'Did Dr Sherback live on the wall?'

Bertha answers like she's ranting to herself. 'Always crawling down the wall like an ugly little beetle – a fart-filled beetle! Always annoying people and telling them what to do. Going on and on about the *insects* and *ecosystems* and why we should be nice to everything or it'll come back to bite us all on the bums. Bet something bit her on the bum. Went looking for the bottom of the wall and never came back. Ha! Good riddance. Nasty old Windy.'

Tabitha imagines what a long drop it would be to the base of the wall.

'Did she fall?' she asks.

Bertha smirks.

'Did she? We'll never know. Maybe she made it to the bottom alive. But one thing's for sure, once we cut her ropes we knew she wasn't coming back. Heh, heh, heh, good riddance, Creepy Windy.'

'You cut her *ropes*?'

* * *

Before the vine net sprouted from the roof of the Plimtocks' house, climbing down the wall was a much more hazardous journey. Dr Sherback used ropes to descend the rock. Each day she climbed further down, adding more bolts and ropes, and when there were enough to take her below the sunline, she set off on her great expedition to the base of the wall.

By this time she had amassed a number of enemies at the edge of the world, Bertha Plimtock among them. They didn't like Dr Sherback's warnings about conserving the plants and the animals around them. Back then the edge was a very different place. The rock wood was a proper wood, with more trees than stones. Wild boar and deer roamed the forest and grazed in green pastures. There was soil and grass, and wheat grew everywhere. There were lakes filled with fish, and bushes filled with nesting birds. The edge was alive with animals and plants, and there were many more human inhabitants than there are now.

But the people overfished the lakes, they stole bird eggs from the nests, they harvested the wheat too early and forced it to grow too fast, and pretty soon the soil got tired. It ran out of nutrients and dried up to dust. When the grass disappeared, so did the animals. The edge became empty and thirsty. Most of the people had to leave.

Dr Sherback predicted it would happen, but nobody believed her. She told them to stop hunting the boar – there weren't enough left – she told them to only take the biggest fish from the lakes, the ones that had already laid eggs. They didn't listen. She went on and on, telling everyone she met what disaster awaited them.

'That bloody doctor,' they'd say, 'doesn't she ever shut up?'

'Found her taking samples from my fields again. Nosey parker. What business is it of hers how I grow my crops?'

'She's downright creepy, don't you think? Crawling about with her magnifying glass and her petri dishes. Gives me the willies.'

So the people on the edge came up with an evil plan. They watched Dr Sherback fixing her ropes to the wall. They heard her talk about her great expedition to the base.

'If she's so fascinated by the base of the wall,' they smirked, 'then she can bloody well stay down there.'

The day after the scientist set off, Bertha Plimtock and some other dreadful human beings crept to the wall and cut the ropes.

'That's the last of her!'

Dr Sherback was never seen again.

* * *

Everybody else is asleep. Tabitha can tell because the bath is vibrating with the snores of all the Plimtocks. She's never been on a train, but she imagines this is what it would be like.

Tabitha can't sleep. She can't stop thinking about poor Dr Sherback. Did she ever make it to the base of the wall? Did she fall? When did she realise her way back up had been sabotaged? Was she still alive, down there, somewhere?

It's no use. Tabitha has to have some answers. She climbs out of the bath and tiptoes downstairs. Taking a slice of leftover cake from the kitchen, she goes to the front room and wafts it under Bertha's nose.

'Hnff, hnff, wha'?' Bertha jolts awake.

'I thought you might be hungry,' Tabitha says, breaking off a piece and shoving it into Bertha's half-asleep mouth.

'Mmm, cake.'

'Bertha?' Tabitha says as the woman sleepily chews. 'Tell me more about Creepy Doctor Windy. Was she really never seen again? Ever, ever?'

'Mmm,' Bertha groans with her eyes closed, 'Belchy Bellows. Idiot.'

'Who is Belchy Bellows?'

'Belchy Bellows saw her in the rock wood.'

Bertha is properly awake now and tips her gaze pointedly at the plate. Tabitha shoves more cake in her mouth and the woman continues.

'Burping fool, Belchy Bellows. Lived in the tree-house beyond the tavern. Saw her several times, he said, only at night, collecting her samples and what-not.'

'This was in the rock wood?'

'Always in the rock wood. Said he chased her once but she vanished, like a ghost. Said it was her coming back from the grave, to take revenge. Revenge on all of us.' Bertha snorts. 'He was full of it though, mad as a hatter. Always telling us to be *kind to the trees*. Kind to *trees*, ha! Fool. He snuffed it not long after she did. Good riddance to him too. Belchy and Windy. The air is fresher without them.'

'Did you ever see the ghost?'

'No such thing as ghosts.' Bertha's eyes are closing

again, and her chewing gets slower.

'Did Belchy Bellows have any relatives?' Tabitha asks. 'Someone who might still be around?'

'Who?' Bertha says.

'Belchy Bellows.'

'Who the hell is Belchy Bellows? And who the hell are you, for that matter? I want some cake! I've been starving all day and no-one will bring me any. What a rotten family I have, letting me die of hunger.'

Tabitha shoves the last of the cake into Bertha's mouth and leaves her be. The woman's memory is gone for the night, and that's all Tabitha is likely to get.

CHAPTER THIRTEEN

DR SHERBACK

In the hall outside the front room, Tabitha wonders if the ghost was real; if Dr Sherback still collects samples at night, if she's still alive and scaling the wall to walk to the rock wood. It would be an awfully long journey – surely an impossible one. Belchy Bellows must have been seeing things.

But curiosity gets the better of Tabitha and she's careful not to slam the front door on her way out. There are little dark bumps around the pond that she presumes to be newts. She waves to them and continues on her way.

The rock wood is a spooky place at night. Tabitha has never seen it in the dark before. She can see twinkling stars through the leaves of the tall trees and, other than the babbling of the stream, there's very little sound. She's not sure where to start in her search for Dr Sherback, so she thinks to herself, *If I was an extremely old woman who was interested in science and insects and creepy crawly things, where would I go?*

She decides she'd stick to the stream. The sound of the water is nice and there are plenty of creatures that crawl in and around the muddy edges. Tabitha follows the winding route through the boulders. The moon is very bright tonight and it throws shadows on the tree trunks. It makes the wood look busy, like there are endless dark figures coming and going, dashing through the trees and behind the stones. She sees a mouse's tail vanish under a bush. She sees cockroaches and tiny fish and squiggling worms. Then she looks up and sees the most enormous insect. It is crouched on a tree trunk very high up, facing downwards. It has huge, blinking, glassy eyes. It holds onto the bark with pale claws that turn into skinny limbs that are attached to a grey-coloured body. The insect isn't just big, it's person-sized. All of a sudden Tabitha realises it's not an insect at all.

She gasps, and the insect-person darts down the tree and runs into the maze of rocks.

'Wait!' Tabitha cries. 'Wait, please!'

The insect-person runs very fast, but Tabitha is also light on her feet. They zigzag through the rock wood until the insect-person leaps over a pool beneath a great big oak tree ... and vanishes. Tabitha can't understand it. Just like that – *poof!* – the insect-person disappears.

'Well,' Tabitha says, 'nothing just vanishes into thin air. You're around here somewhere.'

She climbs the tree and finds nothing. She searches the edge of the pool and finds nothing. She checks the nearby boulders, and nothing. Tired and annoyed, Tabitha plops down in the soft moss at the base of the oak tree. And she sinks, folded in half, up to her knees.

'Ah!' she cries, squeezing herself out like toothpaste from a tube.

She pushes the moss aside and underneath is a tunnel. It's very long and steep – she can't see the end of it.

'Well,' she says, 'if that's where you went, then that's where I'm going.'

Taking a deep breath, she puts both feet into the tunnel and drops. She drops straight onto a mucky slide that goes down and around and down again. She's going so fast her cheeks fill with air and her eyelids feel loose. She slides and slides and slides until – *SCHLIPP* – she soars off the end of the tunnel and bumps to the ground.

'Put 'em up, sunshine,' a voice says. 'You're about to have a very bad day.'

The insect-person is in fact a woman of consid-erable age. Her glassy eyes are actually magnifying goggles that make her real eyes look ginormous. She is older, shorter and paler than Mr Cratchley, yet as she stands in front of Tabitha with her fists raised, she looks formidable. Something about those shrewd, pursed lips says, 'Don't mess with me or I'll pickle your liver and stamp on your toes'.

Tabitha has landed at the base of the slide-tunnel in the most enormous wall pocket she has ever seen. She cannot see where it ends on either side, and the cavern is filled with tables and shelves of jars and bottles and bubbling beakers over bunsen burners. One of Mr Offal's books – *Frankenstein* – featured a doctor who built a person from body parts and brought him to life. This room is what Tabitha imagined his laboratory to look like, though without the mismatched body-part monster.

'Put 'em up,' the goggled woman says again. 'What's the matter, chump, too afraid?'

'Are you Dr Sherback?' Tabitha asks.

'Who wants to know?'

'My name is Tabitha. Tabitha Plimtock.'

'Why would I give a wibblegong's private parts

who you are?' The woman lowers her fists for a moment. 'Hold on, you're not related to that snotty fart-monster Bertha Plimtock are you?'

'Well, yes, sort of.'

'In that case, get those mitts up pronto 'cos I'm about to make short work of you.'

'No, no, you don't understand,' Tabitha says, getting to her feet, 'I'm not here to bother you, I'm here to ask for your help. You are Wendy Sherback, aren't you?'

'So what if I am?'

'A man in the Lonely Tavern told me to find you. He said we'd need the doctor. You see, something's happening on the wall. Animals are disappearing, being gobbled up by strange creatures, and I'm afraid the people will be next.'

The woman lowers her fists to her sides. 'Strange creatures coming to gobble up people, you say? Hmm, well that does change things a bit. Have a seat.'

Tabitha sits at one of the beaker-covered tables

and explains everything. Dr Sherback's giant blinking eyes are disconcerting. The woman makes no comment as she listens, but occasionally sticks her finger in her ear and wiggles it, or taps it pensively on the end of her nose.

'That it?' she says when Tabitha has finished.

'Yes.'

'Hmm.' The woman taps her nose again. 'You seem like a girl who is not particularly stupid, and not particularly unpleasant, so let me ask you this: Are the people on the wall worth saving?'

'Excuse me?'

'Are they worth saving? Would the world be a better place if the people at the edge were to get gobbled up and be no more?'

'No! No, of course not.'

'Hmm,' Dr Sherback says, 'are you sure? Because I had some dealings with that lot once upon a time, and they struck me as particularly stupid and particularly unpleasant. Your Bertha, for instance. She was a rotten little louse. All the Plimtocks back then were rotten little lice.'

Tabitha blushes. She doesn't feel part of the Plimtock family, but she's still ashamed of them.

'It's true that Bertha is not a very nice person,' she says. 'And the younger Plimtocks are … well, they're not very nice either. But there are lots of wonderful people on the wall. Mr Offal lends me his books and gives me fresh eggs to drink, Molly and Richard are the greatest fun, and the wailing twins do worry a lot but they worry for others as much as for themselves. And I'm so afraid for Mr Cratchley. He lives just below the sunline, all on his own. Oh, Dr Sherback, you've no idea how kind and gentle he is. He collects lost love in a jar.'

'Does he?' The woman doesn't look impressed.

'Besides,' Tabitha frowns, 'even those people who are wicked and unkind don't deserve to be gobbled up by the whatever-they-ares. You should help me to save them anyway, because it's the right thing to do.'

This gets a smirk from Dr Sherback.

'Well, aren't you a little do-gooder. Alright then, missy, I will help you. But if truth be told, I've been helping already – at least I've been trying to. You see, I knew this was coming. I tried to warn them back in the day, but they wouldn't listen. And it's much worse than you think it is.'

'What do you mean?' says Tabitha.

'Those sharp-toothed things that have been scoffing goats and geese?'

'What about them?'

The woman narrows her massive eyes. 'They're just the babies.'

CHAPTER FOURTEEN

THE FOOD CHAIN

Wendy Sherback was a very inquisitive child. She couldn't pass a rock without lifting it up and checking what was underneath. She couldn't eat a bowl of her father's curry without separating out the vegetables and slurping the sauce to determine what new ingredient he had added this time to catch her out. She took apart her toys to see how they were made; she experimented on the neighbour children to see how fast the average ten-year-old could run, how high they could climb, how long they could hold their breath underwater. She read books by the dozen and asked questions until she drove her parents and her teachers batty.

Wendy excelled at school and university and became a world-renowned scientist. She studied yaks at the top of Mount Everest and frilled sharks at the bottom of the Mariana Trench. But Wendy's methods were unusual. She tagged birds in mid-flight by dangling off a hot-air balloon ten miles high. She dove into a crocodile-filled river to see what those delicious reptiles got up to beneath the surface. Once, she even crawled into a living nest of deadly army ants to see how they organised attacks on an intruder.

The university that employed Dr Wendy Sherback was very nervous. They got constant complaints about the 'daredevil' scientist who risked death at every opportunity. The director of the board was sweating buckets when a wealthy businesswoman – who gave regular donations to the university – called to say she was currently watching Wendy's legs dangle from the corniced roof above her office window, as the scientist investigated a rare bird that had nested in the gutter. The university wanted rid of Wendy.

They got their chance when Wendy expressed an interest in visiting the edge of the world to study the plants and animals that lived there.

'That's wonderful!' they said. 'Spectacular! Brilliant idea! We're all behind you, Dr Sherback.'

They gave her money to buy as many provisions as she could carry and told her that, should she feel the urge to stay longer at the very edge of the world, they'd be happy to send her more. And that's how Dr Wendy Sherback became a permanent resident at the wall.

'Don't you miss the world?' Tabitha asks.

'Not really,' Dr Sherback replies. 'I mean the flora and fauna were always interesting, but the people were dreadfully dull. Wusses, the lot of them. Scared of everything. Besides, the plants and animals at the edge are so wonderfully weird, I could study them for a hundred lifetimes and never get bored.'

'How long have you been here?'

'Been at the edge now more than seventy years.'

'Seventy years! Wouldn't that make you …'

'Ninety-six years of age.'

'Wow.' Tabitha wonders if she'll still be climbing fit at ninety-six. 'But if you've been here so long, how come I've never met you before?'

'Don't go up the wall,' the woman said, 'just go down.'

'But you do go to the rock wood.'

'At night, to forage for food, steal a few provisions if needs be. That tavern's always open, you know, with those boulder holes in the sides. I use the tunnel to go up; that way I won't be seen, and it's much quicker too.'

'The tavern landlady is quite nice,' Tabitha says. 'If you asked, I'm sure she'd give you some food.'

'I don't deal with those lecherous lepers up there.'

'Why not?'

The woman leans close. 'Because they cut my ropes and left me for dead.'

'Oh.' Tabitha knows the story. 'Yes, but that was a long time ago. Most of the people you knew then are gone. My friends on the wall are good and kind, I promise you.'

The woman only harrumphs in reply so Tabitha changes the subject.

'So, what are the whatever-they-ares?' she says. 'The creatures that are scaling the wall.'

The huge glassy eyes go as wide as they can go and Dr Sherback smiles.

'That would be starting at the end. You wanna learn about the weird and crazy creatures down here, you have to start at the beginning.'

She takes Tabitha through a maze of shelves and tunnels. Tabitha can't believe it – the wall pocket isn't just a massive cavern, it's a warren of corridors and hidden spaces.

'This,' says Dr Sherback, holding up a jar, 'is a squiggly limpet.'

Suspended in some grainy liquid is a shell that

looks like a splat of paint. Inside the shell is something gooey.

'Is that an animal?' says Tabitha.

'A mollusc, like a snail. Take a closer look. It's got a circle of wicked sharp teeth and a raspy tongue. It uses that to scrape algae off the rock.'

Tabitha is fascinated. She never knew snails could have teeth.

'This' – the doctor holds up another jar – 'is a ninja star.'

There had been pictures of starfish in one of Mr Offal's books. The creature stuck to the glass inside the jar looks like them, but it is black and has silver sparkles.

'Wow,' Tabitha says, leaning closer.

Tink. The starfish spins around inside the jar, kicking its five legs to hammer on the glass. *Tink, tink, tink, TINK.* The last kick makes a tiny crack in the jar.

'Take it easy, you,' Dr Sherback says to the animal, and gently puts the jar back on the shelf. 'You gotta watch those ones. Get 'em all riled up and they can take your eye out.'

'Alright.'

'This one's called a ghastly mudslinger.'

The next jar is much larger, and the specimen inside is a creature halfway between a fish and a salamander. It has slimy, smooth skin, big eyes perched on a long head, two spindly legs and a fishy tail. It takes one look at Tabitha and *SPLAT*. It hurls a spindly-handful of muck at the glass.

'The name suits it,' Tabitha says.

'Are you seeing the pattern yet?' asks the doctor.

Tabitha shakes her head. Dr Sherback sighs as if it's obvious.

'The squiggly limpet eats the algae, the ninja star eats the squiggly limpet, and the ghastly mudslinger eats the ninja star.'

'It's the food chain,' Tabitha says.

'Right you are.'

The food chain continues as follows:

vocalisations incl.
hissing, shushing,
wipping and werping

HAMMER-CLAWED
WEASEL

claw

MONSTROUS SPINED
PORCUPINE

reinforced knuckles for
crushing grip on prey

Size: approx.
2x house

FANGED
ATROCITERUS

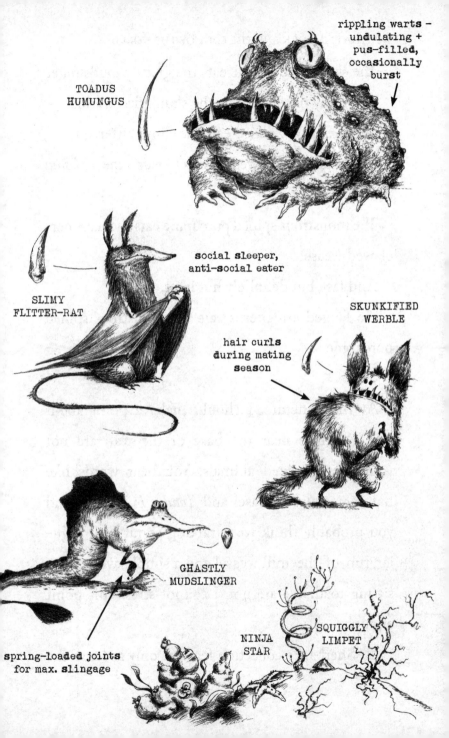

TOADUS
HUMUNGUS

rippling warts –
undulating +
pus-filled,
occasionally
burst

SLIMY
FLITTER-RAT

social sleeper,
anti-social eater

SKUNKIFIED
WERBLE

hair curls
during mating
season

GHASTLY
MUDSLINGER

spring-loaded joints
for max. slingage

NINJA
STAR

SQUIGGLY
LIMPET

The skunkified werble eats the ghastly mudslinger

The slimy flitter-rat eats the skunkified werble

The *Toadus humungus* eats the slimy flitter-rat

The hammer-clawed weasel eats the *Toadus humungus*

The monstrous spined porcupine eats the hammer-clawed weasel

And last, but definitely not least,

the fanged atrociterus eats the monstrous spined porcupine

At this juncture, I should make a point about size. Animals near the base of the wall are not your average-sized animals. You hear words like hammer-clawed weasel and *Toadus humungus*, and you probably think we're talking about your regular, run-of-the-mill weasel and a simple, water-lily-sitting toad. We are not. I cannot stress this point enough.

Dr Sherback's collection features only as far as the

slimy flitter-rat on this particular food chain, and that animal does not fit in a jar. If you or I ever saw a flitter-rat we would think it something like a bat, though much larger, much more leathery and much meaner in the face. A slimy flitter-rat is about the size of a wardrobe. The one in Dr Sherback's lab is stuffed (attempting to keep a live one in captivity would be a profoundly stupid thing to do), but its red, maniacal eyes and sharp teeth are still frightening to behold.

You can imagine that the *Toadus humungus* that feasts on the slimy flitter-rat is considerably larger. (A fascinating natural history note: The *Toadus humungus* fires its sticky, elastic tongue to snap flitter-rats right out of the air as they fly past. It's a magnificent sight to see, if you ever get the chance.) The hammer-clawed weasel that feeds on the *Toadus humungus* is itself quite the monster. The monstrous spined porcupine, you wouldn't want to meet in your worst nightmares, and the fanged atrociterus … well, that's what all the fuss is about, isn't it?

It's possible I've just given you plenty of fuel for bad dreams, and if you're reading this section right before you pop off to sleep, I apologise. It might be best to end the chapter here and pick up the next one tomorrow, in the less scary light of day. Sleep well, and try not to think about flying red-eyed rats and giant fanged monsters.

CHAPTER FIFTEEN

FLIGHT OF THE FLITTER-RAT

A s I mentioned before, the largest animal specimen in Dr Sherback's lab is a stuffed slimy flitter-rat. To represent the larger animals, the scientist has a vast catalogue of hairs, teeth, toenails, snot, etc. Tabitha walks amongst the shelves, captivated. There are stacks of petri dishes with gooey scrapings, and jars of bits that aren't immediately identifiable. The shelves go on and on, but amongst the smaller samples are much larger ones. A single *Toadus humungus* egg is bigger than a beach ball, with a huge black tadpole inside. There's a claw from a hammer-clawed weasel that Tabitha could use to harvest wheat. She stands in awe at the foot of a monstrous spined porcupine's quill and imagines a giant from *Gulliver's Travels* using it to write a letter. And then, the pièce de résistance, set in a glowing algae spotlight in a two-storey alcove, a razor-edged tooth the size of a ship's sail.

'Oh my goodness,' she gasps, 'is that–?'

'A tooth from a fanged atrociterus,' Dr Sherback says from the shadows behind Tabitha, 'and not from one of the biggest either. It's from an adult alright, but a medium-sized one.'

'It's ... it's ...' Tabitha can't find the words.

'Ferocious, is that the word you're looking for? Atrocious? Nail-bitingly terrifying? Yes, it is all of those things. But try picturing that tooth in the wild. Now picture eighty more, packed into a mouth so large it could swallow you whole and not even notice.'

'It's spectacular.'

Tabitha is surprised by her own description. The

animal does sound terrifying, but she can't help feeling wonder that it even exists at all. She notices the doctor smiling at her with her bottle-bottom goggles.

'I see you're a girl after my own heart,' Dr Sherback says. 'Most people would be frightened. Most people would look up at that extraordinary example of nature, pee their pants and run away. Most people wouldn't want to be anywhere near it. But those of us who aren't so easily scared would want to know more. We'd want to see it with our own eyes – see how big it is, how fast it runs, how loud it growls. Some of us would be curious. Are you curious, Tabitha?'

It's the first time Dr Sherback has called her by her name, and Tabitha feels suddenly excited that the scientist may show her even more of the world at the base of the wall.

'I am,' she replies. 'I am curious.'

'Well now,' Dr Sherback's glassy eyes twinkle, 'isn't that something?'

* * *

'Is this safe?'

Tabitha stands at the mouth of Dr Sherback's lab. There's nothing out there but dark. It smells damp and weird.

'Safe?' Dr Sherback says. 'Not in the least. Give your headlamp a shake, girl – it's all that stands between you and oblivion.'

Tabitha wiggles the tiny jar fixed to her forehead by a band, and the bioluminescent algae inside comes to life. The red light doesn't reach very far and isn't very bright.

'The red makes it hard to see,' she says.

'Well, get used to it,' Dr Sherback replies, tapping the jar on her own forehead. 'Animals at the base can't see red light, so you'll see them but they won't see you.'

'What about blue or green light?'

'They see blue and green just fine. Mix up your blue and red algae and you'll be advertising to anything within eyeshot that there's a juicy, stupid morsel here for the scoffing.'

Unlike the top of the wall, the rock near the base is covered with damp and moss. Tabitha finds it almost impossible to get a grip.

'You climb down this all the time?' she asks. 'It's very slippery.'

'We're just going a short distance,' the doctor says, 'then we're going to hitch a lift.'

Tabitha doesn't really like the sound of that. She follows Dr Sherback, who moves like she's taking a morning stroll, and wonders how far a fall it would be if she slipped. Suddenly, the doctor zips up the wall to whisper in her ear.

'I forgot to mention, these things have impeccable hearing, so don't make the slightest sound. I mean it, not a *single* sound.'

What things? The doctor zips back down without elaborating. Tabitha's not sure she can climb without making a single sound. Footsteps are a sound, aren't they? Breathing is a sound. How good is the impeccable hearing these things have?

She hears the slimy flitter-rats before she sees them. It's like a choir of people who can't whistle, trying to whistle. They're all on the edge of broken, high-pitched notes that slip in and out of what's audible, and they're all out of sync. There are flapping leathery sounds too. She sees them then, all hunched together, clinging to the wall with clawed feet so they hang off it at perpendicular angles. While nuzzling their heads together, they look like an extra-large carton of furry, dark eggs. They don't react to the red glow illuminating them from above.

Dr Sherback catches Tabitha's eye, points to the two flitter-rats closest, then mimes jumping with her hand. Tabitha shakes her head roughly. The doctor just nods and mouths, 'On the count of three'. Tabitha shakes her head again but Dr Sherback is holding up one finger, then two fingers. Tabitha's head is shaking like a panicked bobble-head doll when the doctor holds up three fingers and jumps. Even more terrified of being left alone on the wall when the flitter-rats scatter, Tabitha holds her breath and leaps. She lands on the back of a slimy flitter-rat that is more aptly named than it looks. The fur on its back feels oily to the touch, and when it emits a high-pitched squeal and drops off the rock, it's only Tabitha's strong legs that keep her clamped to the animal as it dives and swoops.

'Yeehaw!' Dr Sherback shrieks alongside her, waving one hand in the air and holding fast to her own flitter-rat with the other. 'Ha ha! How's this for a shortcut? Bet old Bertha Fartface never took a ride like this.'

The whole flock of flitter-rats have taken to the air at the same time, and Tabitha can feel the breeze of all their leathery wings as they whoosh past. She's got a grip on two handfuls of the oily fur now and leans low against the back of the flitter-rat's head. The animal has stopped squealing and appears to be ignoring his passenger as he hurtles through the murky dark.

'Where are we going?' Tabitha yells to the doctor.

'They'll take us to the base,' Dr Sherback says. 'There's plenty more to see down there.'

Tabitha's heart is going a mile a minute, but she's starting to enjoy herself now. Suddenly a whole world of adventure has opened its huge, scary mouth and swallowed her whole; it's terrifying and wonderful at the same time.

'Oh, by the way,' the doctor shouts as her flitter-rat pitches to one side, 'beware of *Toadii humungii*. Get ready to jump off if you hear a …'

Her voice trails off as her flitter-rat veers away from Tabitha's.

'What?' Tabitha says. 'Get ready to jump off if I hear *what*?' The doctor disappears into the dark. 'Wait! Where are you going?'

Tabitha tries to steer her flitter-rat but it doesn't seem to work that way. There's no response as she leans left and then right; the animal continues on its own route, oblivious. Fear makes Tabitha want to scream for the doctor, but she thinks drawing unnecessary attention to herself might be a bad idea.

Schlurpp-pp-pp.

The sound comes from below. It's like the sound of someone sucking the very last bit of milkshake through a straw.

Schlurpp-pp-pp.

Tabitha looks around, her red light sweeping over what appears to be the ground below, but she can't see where the sound is coming from.

Schlurpp-pp-pp.

Suddenly, on a rocky hill, an amorphous blob bounds into view. Tabitha sees it just in time to spot the thick, shiny string spring from its mouth.

A *Toadus humungus*!

Without thinking, Tabitha tips to one side and drops from the flitter-rat's back. As she falls she sees the animal snatched from the air by a sticky, elastic tongue.

She hits the ground and rolls to a stop. Tabitha is all alone at the base of the wall, and she has no idea how to get back up.

CHAPTER SIXTEEN

THINGS IN THE DARK

Imagine a sticky, mucky, marshy place. Your feet are slipping one second and getting stuck in mud the next. You watch where you're putting your feet but it's dark. *Very* dark. No moon and no stars kind of dark. The only light is the little red headlamp strapped to your forehead, but the red makes everything that might be a *little* bit creepy look like the opening of a blood-filled horror movie. And there's noise. Slurping, scuttling, shuffling noise. All around. You know what lurks all around you because some loopy, ancient doctor showed you bits of them in her lab. Then that doctor took a joyride on a giant flying rat and left you all alone. Is this sounding like fun yet?

Tabitha doesn't think so. She tiptoes through the muck, trying to be as quiet as possible. She knows the slimy flitter-rats have excellent hearing, but so too might the skunkified werbles or the hammer-clawed weasels or the other wicked-sounding creatures that could be gathering around her right now this second. She has no idea which direction she's going, and there are no stars to lead the way or landmarks other than the wall itself. It's strange that even in the dark she knows it's there. She can feel it somewhere to her right, like a huge shadow, even though it's far too dark for shadows.

She finds a trickle through the muck that grows to a muddy stream, and decides to follow it. Streams always lead somewhere, don't they? After about a hundred metres she hears a *whoo, whoo, whoo, whoo.* She creeps forward, swaying her headlight to and fro, and spots a ninja star, standing on two legs with its other three raised. The three limbs bend as it slowly lifts a leg to balance on one, like a crane pose in karate, then – *whoo whoo whoo* – it spin kicks, knocking a squiggly limpet from the edge of the stream and landing right on top of its shell. *Splat.*

Tabitha smiles. That's an impressive way to catch your dinner. She sees two or three other squiggly limpets on her journey, one skunkified werble that goes scurrying into a hole (she makes a mental note that a skunkified werble walks like its hind legs are always moving faster than its front legs), and she feels the breeze of a passing flitter-rat.

While describing to herself the punk-like strip of hair down the skunkified werble's back, Tabitha realises she forgot to be afraid. The werble is certainly not a small animal, but she was so caught up in seeing something new and weird that she forgot to run away screaming.

Hmm, she thinks, *I must remember to run away next time.*

Not from the werble though. She decides they're not worth the fear factor. Anything bigger and she'll certainly bolt.

And there are bigger things out there. She hears a couple of them now. The giant tooth in the lab rushes to her mind when the sound of something very large scraping against the rock of the wall comes echoing through the red dark. And there's another reason to be afraid. There is luminescent algae up ahead and it's not the red kind. It's blue. Glowing with the kind of light that the animals down here can see. If she steps into that glow, she might as well be in a spotlight.

To keep going, Tabitha has to make a very large circle around the algae patch. As she moves she hears something move with her. She's being followed. It's bigger than a werble and it doesn't have leathery wings. It has soft-sounding footsteps that sometimes click. It's getting closer and closer and closer, until …

'Hi-yah!'

Dr Sherback springs from behind a rock with a

long stick. The stick spins and whacks and cracks and smacks, and something hisses very loudly. Tabitha is knocked to the ground in the scuffle. Lying in the mud she watches an awesome battle between the stick-wielding Dr Sherback and a hammer-clawed weasel. The weasel has a long, furry body that wouldn't fit inside the Lonely Tavern, even if it scrunched up into a tight ball. It has narrow yellow eyes and needly teeth, but the fiercest thing about it is the single curved claw on each of its front paws. They're like scythes that swing and soar and try to slice the doctor in half. Dr Sherback is having none of it.

'Take that!' she yells, striking the weasel hard on the nose. 'And that! And that! And that!'

She reminds Tabitha of the little ninja star and its spin-kicking martial arts. The stick moves so fast it's a blur.

'Want some more?' the doctor yells. 'Not done yet, huh? Then have another' – *POW* – 'and another' – *SMASH* – 'and another!' – *PTAW*.

The hammer-clawed weasel gives one last snarl, then leaps off into the dark, rubbing its nose. Before Tabitha has time to get to her feet, the doctor is standing over her.

'There you are,' she says. 'Was wondering where you'd got to. Flitter-rat took you on a detour, did it?'

'It got eaten by a *Toadus humungus*,' Tabitha says as she is pulled to her feet.

'Yep, that'll happen at the base of the wall. Ready for some more? You're gonna have to employ a little more stealth down here, you know, or you're liable to get gobbled up too. Follow me.'

Still a little dazed, Tabitha follows the doctor as she marches off through the gloomy, muddy dark.

The doctor leads her further and further from the wall. They walk and walk and walk until they come to a ridge. They climb the ridge and Dr Sherback puts her finger to her lips. They keep their tummies to the ground as they peep over the rock.

Tabitha thought she'd been frightened before, but

compared to this moment, that had only been a flutter. Right now, her stomach feels like a heavy bag of live worms, wriggling and squiggling inside her. Beyond the ridge are dozens of mountains. Hills of dark, spiky fur and gleaming white ship sails. But these are not really mountains and hills, and there are no boats among them.

'Behold,' Dr Sherback whispers, 'the fanged atrociterus.'

Each one is twice as big as a house. They pant and drool, and steam rises off them into the chilly air. The steam is like a fog that their wicked eyes glare out from. They snarl at each other, and snap at each other, and each time they do the sharp clatter of giant, razor-edged teeth rings out through the mist. Dr Sherback taps Tabitha's shoulder and points to her right. A clump of mini-mountains sits apart from the giants. They are the babies, and each baby is as big as a car.

The doctor seems enraptured, but Tabitha is too

scared to feel wonder. She tugs on Dr Sherback's sleeve; it's time to leave. As they do, a pebble at Tabitha's foot tumbles down the ridge with a *clack, clack, clack*. The snarling and drooling and snapping stops. Everything is silent. The wriggling worms in Tabitha's tummy go into turbo mode. The beasts beyond the ridge cannot see the red light that shines from the headlamps that the intruders wear, but they know there are intruders. They sniff the air. They move around. They sniff some more and lick their lips. There's something yum and juicy nearby.

Tabitha is paralysed with fear. She's frozen to the spot. She doesn't know what to do until the doctor grabs her by the wrist and they're racing down the ridge.

CHAPTER SEVENTEEN

RUN, RUN, AS FAST AS YOU CAN

It's a funny time to think about snoring – when you're running from a herd of thundering monsters – but that's exactly what crosses Tabitha's mind. The whole world is rumbling with the heavy footsteps of thirty or forty fanged atrociteruses, and it puts her in mind of her bathtub bed, how it trembles and groans with the snoring of four awful Plimtocks. The comparison momentarily distracts her from the mind-numbing fear. But now the fear is back and her legs feel like jelly.

Tabitha is a fast runner, but she's having trouble

keeping up with Dr Sherback. The woman could give an Olympic gold medallist lessons. Her light feet seem barely to touch the ground and never get stuck in the sticky, mucky bits. She keeps a firm hold on Tabitha's wrist, springing from rock to mud to rock, and so far they're staying clear of the sharp teeth.

The monsters behind make a terrible racket. A wave of warm air sweeps over Tabitha – it's from all those gigantic, panting mouths and it smells foul. It smells like rotten fish and rancid meat and dirty, week-old socks. It smells like old eggs and sweaty gym shorts and the very inside of the compost bin. It's almost worse than Bertha's farty beanbag stench.

The doctor seems to know where she is going. She zips over a mucky stream and turns left beyond a boulder. She whips Tabitha clear of a lunging atrociterus and ricochets off a baby monster's back. But no matter how fast they run, the atrociteruses close in.

'We can't outrun them!' Tabitha yells. 'What are we going to do?!'

The doctor points backwards. 'We don't have to outrun *them*' – then she points forwards – 'we just have to outrun *them*.'

She is pointing to a forest of spikes. It takes Tabitha a moment to realise what it is. 'Monstrous spined porcupines!' she cries.

The doctor smiles. 'That's the ticket.'

The porcupines have heard the stampede coming. The forest of spines undulates as they start lolloping away. For a brief moment Tabitha feels sorry for them. That is, until the first spine lands. *WHOOMPH*.

'What was that?'

'Ha ha!' says Dr Sherback. 'That's the porcupines' defence strategy.' Even in the midst of running, the doctor pulls Tabitha in front and points to one of the spiky creatures. 'Watch this one here.'

The porcupine is an awkward runner. She can't possibly outrun the atrociterus. Several of them home in on her and, just before they clamp their teeth onto her tail, she bolts upright and throws her front legs

out to the sides. Four or five spines come loose from her back and spear through the air. An unfortunate atrociterus gets one in the leg. The other spines soar past and plough into the ground – *whoomph, whoomph, whoomph.*

'That's brilliant!' Tabitha cries.

'An ingenious little evolutionary trick,' the doctor agrees. 'But that's all we get to watch for now. It's time for us to bug out.'

Grabbing one of the fallen porcupine spines, Dr Sherback hoofs Tabitha onto her back and pole vaults through the herd of atrociteruses that have now lost all interest in the tiny humans. When clear of the herd, the two of them race across the marshy ground and don't stop until they get to the wall.

'Well, now,' the doctor says, panting, 'how was your first trip to the base of the wall?'

'Incredible,' replies Tabitha and, almost as an afterthought, 'and *terrifying.*'

'All the best trips usually are.'

They follow the wall until the doctor spots a streak of shiny goo. She scoops up handfuls of it.

'Show me your palms,' she says.

'What is that?' asks Tabitha.

'It's *Toadus humungus* mucus.'

'Ew.'

'Snotty and sticky. Wonderful stuff.'

With the mucus smeared on their hands and toes, they are able to climb the wall all the way back to the doctor's lab.

* * *

'You must be very used to running from the monsters down there,' Tabitha says. 'You knew exactly what to do.'

'Practice,' Dr Sherback replies. 'Although it's gotten much less dangerous than it used to be. Once upon a time they really kept me on my toes. Now it's almost too easy.'

'What do you mean?'

The doctor sits opposite Tabitha and puts a jar of glowing algae on the table.

'Did you see any of this down there?' she asks. 'The blue and green stuff?'

'Yes,' says Tabitha, 'there was a patch of blue algae. I remembered what you said about the animals being able to see us in blue light, and I stayed clear of it.'

'One patch?' the woman says. 'One single, solitary patch?'

Tabitha frowns. 'Yes, just the one.'

'Hmm,' says Dr Sherback. 'Seventy years ago it was a very different story. Seventy years ago the base of the wall was lit up like blue-green fire. Pink stuff too, from time to time.'

'Really? Then the animals must have been able to see you all the time.'

'And that's not all,' the doctor says. 'Back then the animals were much more numerous. You see, when the algae was everywhere there were millions of squiggly limpets to eat it. So there were truckloads of ninja stars to eat the limpets. You couldn't take two steps without stepping on a ghastly mudslinger, and there were so many skunkified werbles their mating season was a festival of fights and stand-offs 'cos there weren't enough underground dens to go round.'

'If there was more of everything,' Tabitha says, 'there must have been many more fanged atrociteruses.'

'There were.'

'But if there were lots more, why didn't they come up the wall back then?'

'Because they had a smorgasbord of tasty treats down here,' the doctor explains. 'The food was never-ending. One pod of spined porcupines could number in the hundreds; now you're lucky if there's fifteen or twenty in a group. The environment has changed, the algae has nearly run out and the animals are getting hungry.'

On hearing this, Tabitha asks, 'What does the

algae eat? I mean, if it does eat.'

'That's an excellent question, my dear girl. In most cases throughout the world algae feeds off sunlight, but down at the base–'

'There is no sunlight.'

'None, so the algae actually chows down on detritus that falls from the top of the wall.'

'De-what?'

'Detritus, tiny bits of vegetation. Stuff that falls off when things flower, shed their leaves, et cetera.'

'I see.'

'But since the gormless inhabitants of the edge have over-farmed and over-harvested the place to death, there's not much more than rock and dust there now.'

'So no detritus.'

'The algae doesn't get fed, it starts to die off, and now–'

'There's not enough food in the food chain.'

'Precisely. And desperate times call for desperate

measures. Atrociteruses aren't the greatest parents in the world. The adults eat first and, if there's any left over, the babies get the scraps. It's the babies that get hungriest first, so it's the babies that are climbing the wall in search of goats and geese.' Dr Sherback sighs. 'I thought I was keeping a proper eye on things, that I'd notice when it really took a turn for the worse. But those babies must have snuck right past me – I'd no idea they were climbing the wall til you plonked your bottom on my laboratory floor.'

'If the food is still running out,' Tabitha says, 'will the adults start climbing too?'

'Oh yes,' the doctor replies, 'and it's not just everyone at the edge of the world that's at risk. If those beasts get a taste for human meat there are billions more for the taking. If the atrociteruses find themselves a habitat that suits, they could eat and eat and multiply and eventually overrun the entire planet.'

'Oh my goodness!'

'This is what happens,' says Dr Sherback, 'when

things get out of whack. I warned those people seventy years ago. They wouldn't listen and now look what's happened – we're all going to get gobbled up by giant, drooling monsters.'

CHAPTER EIGHTEEN

PARCELS FOR PROTECTION

It's near morning as Tabitha walks through the rock wood. Her visit to the base of the wall seems almost like a dream, or a nightmare – she can't decide which. The journey back up the slide from Dr Sherback's laboratory was easier than she expected. A pulley system fixed to the roof of the tunnel meant she could clip herself onto one rope, pull on the other and glide up the slide with very little effort. She is exhausted after such a wild night of adventure though, and she's wondering if she can sneak in an hour's sleep before she has to get up and make Gower's fat-free, dairy-free, wheat-free breakfast.

She's so sleepy that it's not until she's in view of the house at the edge of the cliff that she notices the train behind her. It's like a river of red and purple and sparkly, spotty stripes.

'Shoo,' she says, 'shoo, go home.'

The number of newts in the pond has already grown considerably – they are frequently climbing the garden fence and wriggling through the grass – but now a swarm of them has followed her from the rock wood. Tabitha is perplexed.

'You can't be here,' she says. 'They won't like it.'

The newts don't move. They stand on their hind legs and stare at her.

'Gower will grill you,' she says, 'and Gristle will smack you with the flat of her spade. And that's nothing compared to what Cousin Wilbur will do. He has a rotten temper.'

The newts don't move. They stand and stare.

Tabitha has no choice but to head into the house and hope that they'll go away on their own.

She tiptoes up the stairs to the bathroom, takes off her slightly damp jumper and rolls it up to rest her head on it. Just an hour's sleep will do the trick. One hour so she doesn't feel so exhausted.

'Cake!' comes the shriek from below. Bertha is up early. 'It's my birthday and not one of my rotten relatives bothers themselves to bake me a cake. What selfish, ugly things you are! What snivelling, careless creatures. I want my birthday cake. Bring me birthday cake!'

Tabitha crawls out of the bath and puts her jumper back on.

* * *

'Oooh, what fresh hell invades our nightmarish existence!' Merry Lost hangs halfway out the window of her wooden shack, her long black hair flowing in the

wind. 'What ravenous beast crawls from the depths to feed on the shadowy meat of our sorrow!'

'Morning, Merry.'

Tabitha has come straight to the wailing twins' shack with the day's shopping list. But she is looking for more than her regular shopping. In her pocket is a recipe of Dr Sherback's.

'This is not foolproof, you hear?' the doctor had said. 'If an atrociterus is determined to eat you, then this stuff won't do much. But they don't like the smell – far too sweet for them – and if there are other smells on the wind, they just might decide to leave you alone. Lavender, cinnamon and honeysuckle. Know anyone who grows that sort of stuff?'

Tabitha does. The wailing twins grow lots of herby plants and sweet things.

'Where's Jerry today?' Tabitha asks the limp body hanging out of the window.

'Oooh, woe is me!' Another body flops out the other window to hang over the sill.

'Oh,' says Tabitha, 'there he is. Hello, Jerry. How are you?'

'We are distraught,' Jerry replies.

'Oh dear.'

'The world is ending,' cries Merry.

'That does sound serious.'

Jerry cups his face with his hands in horror. 'The harbinger of doom peeked through our window last night.'

'Goodness,' Tabitha says, 'did he?'

'And now we fear the world must end in a fiery blaze of, of ... of fire,' says Merry.

'That doesn't sound like fun.'

'Those wicked eyes,' Jerry says.

'That steaming, sizzling fur,' Merry says.

'That mouth filled with teeth like enormous kitchen knives!'

Tabitha suddenly pays attention. The harbinger of doom sounds awfully familiar.

'It peeked through your window last night?' she asks.

'Yes,' says Jerry, 'and breathed on the glass. We held up our hands against it and ordered it to leave this realm.'

'Which it did,' Merry says proudly.

Tabitha glances at the windowsills, inside and out. There are pots of growing lavender and, hanging from the curtain rails, bunches of drying honeysuckle.

'You two,' she says, 'are the luckiest siblings ever.'

'But woe are we!' cries Jerry.

'Yes, yes, woe are you. Is it alright if I come in? I have a special order for you.'

* * *

Tabitha has commissioned the twins to make a number of special parcels – small bags of lavender, cinnamon and honeysuckle, as many as they can make. While the twins get to work, she goes in search of Richard and Molly. She finds them sitting on a rocky outcrop, looking forlorn.

'Three more,' Richard says when Tabitha asks. 'Three more went missing last night.'

'We've been trying to herd the rest of the goats into wall pockets,' says Molly, 'to keep them as safe as we can, but they're not willing.'

'It's like herding cats,' Richard says, 'cats who bleat in your face and don't like small spaces. Goats are such idiots.'

Several of the animals stand dotted on the wall around the outcrop. They turn their faces to the sun, taking deep, meditative breaths. Tabitha doesn't think they're idiots; it seems to her they'd simply rather take their chances on the wall than submit to living in a rocky cage. Goats value their freedom above all else. They can never truly be tamed.

'Molly, Richard,' Tabitha says, 'I know what it is that's been eating your goats.'

Tabitha tells them everything. She tells them about Dr Sherback and the base of the wall, about the food chain and the disappearing algae. She tells them about her ride on the back of a flitter-rat and using the monstrous spined porcupines to escape a thundering herd of fanged atrociteruses.

'So the doctor's going to help us,' Tabitha says. 'As much as she can, anyway.'

'She's still *alive*?' Molly says. 'She must be a hundred.'

'Ninety-six, but that doesn't seem to have slowed her down at all.'

'Tabby, love,' Richard says, 'how do you know you can trust this woman? I mean, you've only just met her. And I have to say, I don't like that she took you on such a dangerous journey, where you nearly got eaten alive by fanged atrops-alotterisses.'

'Fanged atrociteruses.'

'Fanged whatever-they-ares. I don't like this one little bit, sweetheart. It all sounds very unsafe to me.'

'Well,' Tabitha considers, 'it is very unsafe. But if we just ignore it, we'll all eventually be eaten by fanged atrociteruses anyway. And not just us – maybe someday, the entire world. We've got to do something about it.'

'But what are we supposed to do?' Molly asks.

'We can start small. Dr Sherback gave me a recipe for protective bags to hang outside your door and around your neck. In fact, the twins should be nearly finished making them by now.'

* * *

'Last one,' Merry says, dropping a little cotton bag into a sack on the floor.

'And you kept some for yourselves?' Tabitha says.

'On every window and over the door,' Jerry replies, 'but our entreaties to the beast were more effective. We asked him to leave this realm, and he did.'

'Unfortunately he didn't quite leave this realm, he just ate a goat instead.' Tabitha throws the sack over her shoulder. 'I'm very grateful for all your work, thanks very much. Be careful, won't you?'

'And you' – Merry puts a hand on her arm – 'for I fear dark forces follow you, my dear Tabitha. Yes, yes, I can sense a great power following your aura.'

'I sense it as well.' Jerry suddenly closes his eyes and raises his hands to the air. 'Yes, Merry, you are quite correct. A great power following you … like a lost puppy.'

Tabitha waits until Jerry peeks open one eye.

'Okey doke,' she says, 'I'll watch out for that. Thanks again, you two.'

Stepping out onto the porch, Tabitha stops short. Lined up along the wall as far as she can see are Richard and Molly's goats. They seem to be queueing for something. Richard and Molly stand on the other side of the porch, looking dumbfounded.

'Tabby, sweetheart,' Richard says, 'what did you do?'

'Nothing,' Tabitha replies. 'I told you, goats are smarter than you think.'

CHAPTER NINETEEN

THE ATTACK ON MR CRATCHLEY

Tabitha hangs a lavender parcel around the neck of each goat. Once furnished with a cotton bag, each goat trots off and the next one in the queue comes forward. Richard and Molly watch in fascination.

'I told you they were smart,' Tabitha says.

'Hmm,' Richard says, not sounding convinced.

When Richard, Molly and all their goats have been given lavender parcels, and after she has dropped some in to Mr Offal, Tabitha begins her descent to visit Mr Cratchley. When she steps off the vine net and is climbing below the sunline, she feels movement in her rucksack. Swinging the bag off her shoulders, she mooches around inside and nearly falls off the wall when a red head pops out.

'Goodness,' she says, 'what are you doing in here?'

It must have crawled into her bag before she left the house, but she can't imagine why. The newt blinks at her with its pale eyes, then crawls up her arm and into her hair.

'Hey!' Tabitha says. 'Get out of there.'

But the creature won't be moved. It sits facing out, holding position by grabbing bunches of her hair, and watches the darkness behind her.

'Well,' she says, giving up on trying to force it back into the rucksack, 'if you see anything out there with sharp teeth, let me know.'

'What is that?' says Mr Cratchley when she arrives at his wall pocket.

'A newt,' says Tabitha.

The man looks distinctly uncomfortable. 'I didn't

know you had a newt for a pet.'

'It's not a pet, it's a nuisance. How are you today, Mr Cratchley?'

'Oh, I'm very well, thank you,' he says, keeping a nervous eye on the newt.

'Did anything happen during the night?'

'Like what?'

Tabitha sighs and explains how more goats have gone missing. She tells him about Dr Sherback and the base of the wall too.

'Oh, I don't like you going all the way down there,' he says, pulling anxiously on the cuff of his sleeve. 'I wish you wouldn't go down there again. I don't want anything bad to happen to you.'

'Neither do I,' Tabitha says, walking to the back of the wall pocket. 'Your lost love is very bright today.'

'It is,' he agrees. 'Please don't go down the wall again.'

'I might have to, but it's for the best. If Dr Sherback and I can do anything to keep you and the others safe, we're going to do it.'

Mr Cratchley blinks his watery eyes. 'I would be very unhappy if something bad were to happen to you. Very unhappy.'

Tabitha smiles. 'I'll be alright. Could I have a glass of water? I climbed quite far today.'

He jumps and rushes to get a glass. 'Of course, of course, how thoughtless of me. You must be very thirsty.'

Tabitha keeps hold of the jar of lost love as they sit and chat. As she talks of her adventures Mr Cratchley becomes more and more fidgety. She changes the subject, but he remains dreadfully nervous. Finally, Tabitha hands him the jar, keeping hold of it for a moment so they're very close.

'I promise I'll be careful,' she says.

'Okay.'

'I'll be alright. We all will.'

'Okay.'

Tabitha stays much longer than she normally

would. It's past sunset, and the Plimtocks will be screaming for their dinner, but she wants to see Mr Cratchley calm before she leaves. They go through his collection of strange items, and she asks him questions she has asked him a hundred times before. When she finally grabs her rucksack, having convinced the little newt to crawl back inside, both she and Mr Cratchley are feeling much better.

'Take care, Tabitha,' he says. 'I hope to see you soon.'

She waves goodbye and starts to climb up the wall. She's nearly reached the vine net when she gets an eerie feeling. She looks down but can't see anything, it's too dark. In the pocket of her rucksack, she finds the red algae headlamp that Dr Sherback gave her. She gives it a shake and holds it low. The red algae lights up and she can see just as far as Mr Cratchley's. A black shape is moving near the wall pocket. In the dark, it looks black and hairy. Gasping, Tabitha pulls the lamp onto her head and starts climbing back down.

* * *

She's in such a hurry, she doesn't look down as she climbs. The lavender parcels hanging in Mr Cratchley's doorway must have done the trick – the baby atrociterus decides to go for something else; something a little further up the wall, something it can smell.

Sniff, sniff.

Tabitha freezes.

Sniff, sniff.

She looks down and gets a noseful of its sweaty-sock breath. In the red glow she can see its nostrils flaring as it sniffs and sniffs and sniffs. Then it grins with huge kitchen-knife teeth. The mouth opens wide and,

SNAP.

The atrociterus misses but Tabitha falls from the wall. She is tumbling and spinning until,

snap.

A strong, cold hand clamps around her wrist and she is hanging in the air at the doorway of Mr Cratchley's wall pocket.

'It's right above us,' Tabitha whispers.

Moving quickly, Mr Cratchley carries her inside, all the way to the back of the room, and hides her behind a stack of shelves.

'What are you going to do?' she asks.

'I'm going to distract it.'

'How?'

He doesn't reply but hangs a silk scarf on the shelves to keep her hidden. Tabitha peeks out as best she can and is flummoxed to see him standing right in the middle of the room, in the light of the blue and green algae.

'What are you doing?' she whispers.

He turns and puts a finger to his lips.

'If it eats me,' he says, 'then it won't be hungry any more. You must be quiet, however.'

His wrinkled hands are shaking as he clasps them

to his chest and turns back to face the doorway. Tabitha is about to yell at him to hide when a pair of eyes, like a pair of crescent moons, appears at the doorway and her blood runs cold. She is too afraid to move.

'Hello,' Mr Cratchley says. His entire body is shaking now but he doesn't move from his spot on the floor. 'Goodness, those are large teeth. I think I'm destined to be your dinner this evening, and I'd be very grateful if the whole thing were to happen rather quickly. Very grateful, indeed.'

The atrociterus barely fits through the doorway. Drool drips from its fangs into puddles on the ground. It opens its mouth and lunges at the polite man in the middle of the room.

'No!'

Tabitha springs from her hiding place and knocks the old man aside. The monster bites down on nothing and is furious. It lunges again and Tabitha and Mr Cratchley roll out of its way; the animal crashes

into shelves and lots of precious things are broken.

'Oh, goodness,' Mr Cratchley says, breathing fast, 'oh no.'

'Run, Mr Cratchley!'

Tabitha pulls him around the wall pocket as the atrociterus slams into one lot of shelves, then the next, then the next. All the while, Mr Cratchley is gasping, 'Oh dear, oh no. Oh goodness, no. Not my ... oh no.'

He is knocked aside by one clawed paw and the monster stands over Tabitha. There is no escape. She closes her eyes, waiting for the inevitable, and suddenly smells another smell underneath the sweaty breath of the atrociterus. It's a fresh smell, like a summer meadow. She opens her eyes; the monster isn't lunging. The red newt has crawled from Tabitha's rucksack and is now clinging to the atrociterus's snout, looking back at Tabitha and blinking its pale eyes. The monster seems bewildered by the scent wafting from the amphibian's skin. Then the monster seems sleepy. Its head nods up and down, up and down, and it smiles like the way you smile when you remember your mother reading you a bedtime story. Then finally,

FLUMP.

It lands in a heap on the floor and snores. The wall pocket shakes with the fall, and the jar of lost love – the only surviving item of Mr Cratchley's collection – tips to one side and rolls off its shelf.

'Oh no,' the man's soft voice comes from one corner.

But Tabitha is the best goalie the world has never seen. She leaps over the beast on the floor and dives to the ground beyond it, catching the jar safely on her belly. The lost love inside twinkles.

CHAPTER TWENTY

CHAINED TO THE KITCHEN SINK

I t is morning before Tabitha makes it back to the house at the edge of the cliff. It took a lot of cajoling to convince Mr Cratchley to leave the shattered remains of his collection and climb above the sunline, despite the sleeping baby atrociterus in the middle of his floor. Tabitha settled him uncomfortably in the wailing twins' shack, but she suspects he may need moving after a while – no-one could be expected to listen to the wailing of the twins for days on end without losing their mind.

She is exhausted when she steps from the net to

the windowsill and into the bathroom. She'd love to have a quick lie-down and rest her weary limbs, but there's no time to lose; she has to tell Dr Sherback about the newt and its strange fresh-meadow smell and how it made the atrociterus sleepy.

At the bottom of the stairs, however, a huge, orange-haired orangutan is waiting for her. He grabs her with his thick, muscly arms and bounds towards the kitchen.

'Cousin Wilbur,' Tabitha cries, 'please let me go. I have a very important message I have to deliver.'

'You have a very important breakfast you have to make, you lazy snotrag. How *dare* you.'

Gower and Gristle stand in the kitchen with their arms folded.

'Yeah,' says Gristle, 'how bloody dare you. Sneaking off for the whole night. Bertha had one of her screaming fits – we had to listen to that for hours. We got no dinner and now we've got no bloody breakfast!'

'You're taking liberties, you rotten little insect,' Gower says. 'It's about time you learned your place.'

'What do you mean?' asks Tabitha.

Cousin Wilbur grins. He holds her upside down with one large, leathery hand. In his other there is suddenly a manacle – a metal ring that he clamps shut around her ankle. The metal ring is attached to a pipe beneath the kitchen sink by a long chain.

'This is what we mean,' he says. 'We've given you far too much freedom, and look how you've repaid us. Well, from now on, you malodorous pimple, you will stay in the house where you belong.'

'But ... but' – Tabitha wriggles in the air – 'you don't understand! The whole wall's in trouble, the whole *world's* in trouble. If I don't get to Dr Sherback–'

The orangutan shakes her so hard she might have thrown up her breakfast had she eaten any.

'The wall's in trouble,' Cousin Wilbur mimics her, 'the world's in trouble ... Like we'd care even if it was.'

Then Tabitha thinks of an excellent point.

'How will you get cider and eggs and milk,' she says, 'if I can't leave the house?'

'She thinks she's got us,' Gristle sneers.

'Like we're that stupid,' says Gower. 'We've got that sorted, you little snot. For the cider, I'll jog to the tavern each morning instead of jogging on the spot.'

'And as for everything else,' Cousin Wilbur says, 'we've got a much longer chain in the cupboard under the stairs. Anytime we want something, we'll hook it to your ankle, hang you off the cliff and swing you from side to side.'

'In fact, it's more efficient,' says Gower. 'No waiting for you to crawl your way down like a limping beetle, or have you waste more time by chatting and schmoozing and making friends. And if you do try any of that rubbish, we can give the chain a shake, or swing you somewhere else.'

'Or drop you altogether.' Cousin Wilbur is grinning again. 'I don't know why we never thought of this before. It's a stroke of genius.'

'What is that?!' Gristle suddenly shrieks.

The newt that snuck into Tabitha's rucksack has apparently been hiding in her jumper since leaving Mr Cratchley's wall pocket. It pokes its small head out from under the wool.

'It's a slimy lizard!' says Gower.

'Kill it, kill it!' cries Gristle.

Cousin Wilbur smacks an orangutan hand hard on Tabitha's back.

'You missed,' Gower says. 'Whack her again, whack her again!'

'No, it's on the floor!' Gristle leaps onto the kitchen table. 'It's one of those horrible slimy things from the pond.'

'It's a newt,' Tabitha says, getting her breath back from all the shaking and hitting, 'and it's harmless. Let me go and I'll put it out the door.'

'Kill it, kill it!' Gower is now also standing on the table.

Cousin Wilbur kicks at the newt with his long, hand-like feet, but the animal makes him nervous. It walks with a weird scuttling walk, swinging its tail from side to side. Scuttling out the kitchen door, it disappears into the front room.

'Aaaaagghhh!' Bertha's scream makes the walls shake. 'Get it off me, get it off me! There's a beastly little thing on my beanbag. Somebody get in here and squash it!'

Tabitha is still hanging upside down in the kitchen.

'Let me go,' she says to Cousin Wilbur, 'and I'll catch it.'

Snarling, the orangutan drops her to the floor and she hurries into Bertha's room. The woman has rolled off her beanbag, letting its few days of stench waft into the air. She points at the bag and screams.

'Squash it! There it is. Squash it, squash it!'

Tabitha quickly cups the red and purple newt in her hands. The orangutan stands at the door, holding a frying pan.

'Give it here and I'll squish it,' he says, but Tabitha hurries to the window instead.

Cousin Wilbur steps on her chain and she falls short. The newt goes flying through the air and smacks onto the glass with its sticky feet. Before Cousin Wilbur can get to it, the amphibian escapes through the slightly open window. The orangutan turns around with flashing eyes.

'You bring one of those nasty little creatures into our house ever again and I'll squish it. And after I'm done squishing it, I'll squish *you*.'

'Hear, hear,' says Gristle from the doorway.

'Now get into the kitchen,' Gower says, 'and make the breakfast.'

***

In between making the meals and making an eggless birthday cake and cleaning the whole house from top to bottom, Tabitha tries her best to pick the lock on the manacle around her ankle, but it's no good. She's stuck.

The chain doesn't stretch comfortably to the bath, so she sleeps in the kitchen sink. The table might be more comfortable, but she's so used to sleeping in the bath that she has trouble dozing off without a tap nearby. Being a light sleeper, Tabitha wakes to a tiny *tap, tap, tap* from the front room just as dawn is beginning to break. She tiptoes past Bertha, carrying the chain so it doesn't drag along the floor, and spots a pair of huge, glassy eyes at the window.

'Dr Sherback!' Tabitha whispers and rushes to open the window.

'You were a no-show last night and again tonight,' the doctor says. 'Scared you off after all, did I?'

'Shh! You have to keep your voice down. Bertha's asleep over there, on the beanbag.'

Dr Sherback looks past her to the sleeping woman, then wrinkles her nose.

'As rosy-smelling as ever, I notice.'

'I'm very sorry I haven't been back. I meant to yesterday, but look' – Tabitha holds up the chain – 'they've locked me into the house, I can't get out.'

'Those rotten fiends! Those Plimtocks really are as nasty as ever. Tell me who's got the key and I'll beat it out of them.'

'Oh no, please don't. Cousin Wilbur is an orangutan at the moment, and he's awfully strong. I'm afraid you'd get hurt, then who would look out for the atrociteruses?'

The woman's eyes darken.

'That's actually what I came to see you about,' she says. 'I think we've reached zero hour.'

'What do you mean?'

'I've just come from the base and there's some fierce scuffling going on down there. The lack of food has reached crisis point and I don't think they'll last another night. The adults are going to scale the wall. The *real* monsters are coming.'

CHAPTER TWENTY-ONE

OLD ENEMIES

Tabitha's ears are ringing. One more day and monsters twice as big as this house, with teeth the size of ships' sails, could be crawling all over the edge.

'Are you sure?' she says, trembling.

'Oh yes,' says Dr Sherback. 'What I saw tonight was a definite shift in behaviour. There's too many of them for too little food; either they'll rip each other apart or they'll simply climb the wall. And Tabitha, my dear girl, there's not a whole hell of a lot we can do about it.'

'Wait,' says Tabitha, 'there might be. That's what I needed to tell you. Mr Cratchley was attacked last night–'

'That old bloke you're so fond of?'

'Well, he's a good bit younger than you, but yes, him. A baby atrociterus came into his wall pocket and tried to gobble us up.'

'Holy spawning waterlouts! It's a wonder you're still alive.'

'That's the thing, there was a newt in my rucksack.'

'A newt?'

'In my rucksack,' says Tabitha.

'Why'd you have a newt in your rucksack?'

'It snuck in.'

'Now that's right strange. Did it crawl in there from here? Was it in the house?'

Tabitha shakes her head. 'It doesn't matter how it got in there, the point is it let off this smell.'

'What kind of smell? Something like Bertha, the giant rotting louse over there?'

'No, no, a nice smell; fresh, kind of like the outdoors in summer. Like green grass and fresh air and sunshine.'

'Blimey, that's an aspirational little amphibian.'

'And it made the atrociterus sleepy,' Tabitha says, 'and a minute later it passed out.'

'Unconscious?' asks the doctor.

'Yes, but not like it got hit on the head, more like it fell into a nice sleep. I think it was smiling.'

'I'd imagine that was an unsettling sight, and an interesting one.'

'Yes, but what do you think happened?'

'Well,' says Dr Sherback, 'there are plenty of amphibians that secrete dangerous chemicals through their skin – you don't wanna go touching poison dart frogs, for instance – but I'm less familiar with one that lets off a summery smell that makes monsters sleep. Did the fumes have any effect on you or that old bloke?'

'No,' Tabitha says, 'Mr Cratchley and I were fine.'

'That is fascinating. Species-specific maybe. What kind of newt was it?'

'It was dark red and purple. I've been seeing a lot

of them lately. In fact, I've been seeing a whole lot of newts lately – there's a load of them around the pond, and plenty in the rock wood too.'

'I have noticed an increase in sub-species on my nightly visits to the rock wood, alright,' the doctor says. 'Colours and patterns I haven't seen before.'

'Do you think they can all produce the summery smell?'

'No way of knowing,' Dr Sherback replies, 'but this is a very interesting development. Good work, Tabitha.'

Tabitha blushes. 'So how can we use–'

'Nnn-whazzat?' A sleepy voice says from the back of the room. 'Who … What the …?' Bertha is fully awake and her eyes narrow. '*Creepy Doctor Windy.*'

'Bertha, you foul windbag,' Dr Sherback says through the window.

'You're still alive.'

'Alive and kicking, in spite of you and your wretched cronies. I see time hasn't been kind, Bertha. You were a twisted, foul being way back then, and you're even more twisted and foul now.'

'Interfering old wench,' Bertha snaps.

'Is that the best you can do? I'm standing here after seventy years, my nostrils burning with the stench of your intolerable digestive system, and that's the worst you can do?'

'Festering busybody, I should've cut your ropes sooner. Evidently you didn't fall far enough.'

Tabitha tries to shush the doctor, but the doctor won't be shushed.

'Tried to murder me and you couldn't even get that right.' Dr Sherback's face is getting very red. 'You're useless and worthless and putrid and foul. You're lazy and greedy, self-centred and slimy. You're everything that's wrong with the world, Bertha. You sum up humankind's worst excesses in one gaseous, self-ish, devious person. We all stand on a precipice, you floundering glutfish, and people like you are going to push us over the edge.'

'As haughty as ever, you snobbified blob.' Bertha is nearly rolling off her beanbag in anger.

'You wafting windbag!'

'You snot-filled toe rag!'

'You pus-ridden whale wart!'

'You maggot-infested blister!'

Tabitha's attempts to shush both women go ignored until, finally, Bertha lets out a shriek loud enough to wake the dead.

'*Get this withered old harpy out of my house!*'

There is the thump of two primate feet on the floor above.

'Dr Sherback,' Tabitha hisses, 'you have to go!'

'And leave you here with these wretched bruise-bags? I will not.'

'You have to! That's Cousin Wilbur coming down the stairs.'

'Well,' the doctor says, crawling through the window and putting up her fists, 'if he's the mindless chump who clamped that thing around your ankle,

I'll be glad to meet him.'

Tabitha silently begs for a miraculous change in the wind, but when Cousin Wilbur enters the room he's still a huge, orange-haired ape. At the sight of him Dr Sherback seems momentarily worried, but she quickly recovers, rolling her fists in preparation for a fight.

'This clever young girl,' she says to Cousin Wilbur, 'is coming with me. So hand over the key to that chain and we'll say no more about it.'

The orangutan chuckles.

'Please get out of here, Doctor,' Tabitha whispers, 'before you get hurt.'

The doctor snorts. 'I've taken on bigger monsters than him, my dear, don't you fret. Come on, Wilfred, or whatever your name is, let's see what you've got.'

Under most circumstances no-one could outfox, outrun or outthink Dr Wendy Sherback, but in the confined space of the Plimtocks' front room the muscled orangutan has the advantage. He snatches her leg and she punches his nose. He grabs hold of her arm and she whip-kicks his belly. She hammers his head and kicks at his shins. She pokes at his eye and leaps over his head. But no matter how many hits the doctor gets in, the great ape doesn't falter. Finally, he grabs hold of her hair and heads for the front door.

Tabitha hooks her hands around his ankle; Cousin Wilbur doesn't notice and she is dragged along the floor until the chain snaps tight and she is pulled from his leg as he steps through the door. Outside, the morning sun is beating down.

'You're a Plimtock alright,' the doctor yells, still hanging by her hair, 'you foul beast!'

The orangutan just sniffs, then swings the doctor around and around and around and around, letting go so she goes soaring through the air, over the fence, past the pond and all the way to the rock wood.

'You rotten louse!' The doctor's voice trails off as

she plummets into the trees in the distance. 'I'll be *baaaaack*.'

Cousin Wilbur storms back into the house and pokes a finger in Tabitha's cheek.

'You,' he says, 'are going to pay for waking me up so early *and* for bringing some wrinkled weirdo into our house. Get cooking the breakfast sharpish, or I'll drop you off the roof.'

Tabitha feels helpless as she puts two slices of bread in the toaster. She's worried about Dr Sherback, but she's also worried about the fanged atrociteruses. They'll be crawling up the wall tonight and nothing is going to stop them.

Gazing out through the kitchen window, through the thick green strands of the vine net, she thinks of Mr Cratchley and everyone else who'll soon be at the mercy of hungry beasts. A plan starts to form, but Tabitha looks down at her feet and frowns. If she is to be of any use to anybody, she has to break free of that chain.

CHAPTER TWENTY-TWO

A LONG WAIT

Before lunchtime Tabitha hears an odd sound coming from the front garden.

'*Pssst, pssst.*'

It's a very quiet noise that sounds between bouts of Bertha's midday snores.

'*Pssst, pssst.*'

Tabitha drags her chain through the hall and puts her ear to the door.

'Hello?' she whispers.

'*Pssst, pssst*, it's me.'

'Dr Sherback!'

Gower has gone for a run after his jog, and Gristle and Cousin Wilbur are somewhere upstairs. Tabitha checks to make sure no-one is coming, then quietly opens the door.

'Dr Sherback, I'm so glad you're alright, but you can't be here.'

'I'm sorry I let that undergrown gorilla get the better of me,' the doctor says, 'but we don't have time for this now. Here's a paperclip and a screwdriver – try and get that thing off your leg. In the meantime, I've been herding newts.'

'Herding newts?'

'Yes, but the blasted things won't be herded.' Dr Sherback looks frazzled as she pulls a single bright-blue newt from a bag over her shoulder. 'Been at it all bloody morning and this is the only one I could catch. I tried to crowd a bunch of them together but they're nimbler than gymnastic fleas. I mean, I catch mudslingers and ninja stars with no bother, for good-ness sake. Who'd have thought newts would be so bloody difficult?'

'Oh, no.'

'And that's not all,' the doctor says, giving the newt a little squeeze so he wriggles. 'I've no idea how to get them to squirt that summery stuff. Look at this fella, he's got to be ticked off with me by now, but' – she holds the newt to her nose and takes a long sniff – 'nothing.'

'Maybe they only do it around atrociteruses.'

The woman stops sniffing.

'That's a good point. Perhaps newts and atrociteruses appeared at the same time and didn't gel – one was too bitey and the other too smelly – leading to an evolutionary arms race that left the little critters at the top of the wall and the great beasts at the bottom.' She frowns. 'It's a dangerous assumption to make though – if you're facing a raging stampede of fanged atrociteruses, you'd want to be sure these newts are going to do their summery scent thing.'

'I don't think we can be sure.'

Dr Sherback puts the blue newt back in her bag.

'You're a clever girl, Tabitha. I nearly forgot the

most important thing a scientist needs to have, and you've reminded me of it.'

'What's that?'

'Pluck, my dear girl,' the doctor says, hurrying away, 'a bit of pluck. I'm gonna get these newts, and they're going to save the day.'

'Good luck, Dr Sherback,' Tabitha says, waving.

'Get that thing off your leg, missy,' the doctor calls back, 'and come find me in the rock wood. I'll be needing all the help I can get!'

Tabitha smiles before the door is slammed shut by a large, leathery hand. Cousin Wilbur, still the dark-eyed orangutan, stares her down until her knees feel wobbly.

'Told you she was skiving off down there.' Gristle stands at the top of the stairs with folded arms.

'I see that old bag one more time,' Cousin Wilbur growls in Tabitha's face, 'and I'll throw her off the edge. Got that, you feeble slug?'

'Yes, Cousin Wilbur.'

'Now go get my lunch ready.'

'And when you're done with that, you can tidy my bedroom,' Gristle says. 'I can't find any clean underwear in all that rubbish. I've been wearing the same pair for a week.'

Tabitha grimaces at the idea of touching anything in Gristle's disgusting bedroom, but she doesn't complain. She makes Cousin Wilbur's lunch and thinks through her plan. It's a good one, she thinks – especially as Dr Sherback is having such a difficult time trying to collect newts – but it will require a bit of luck, a lot of speed, and she can only attempt it very late in the evening. That's the worst part – the waiting. And if the plan doesn't work, there'll be nothing to stop the atrociteruses climbing all the way to the top of the wall.

* * *

Tabitha has tried the paperclip in the lock at her

ankle – it's too thin and bendy. She has tried the screwdriver – it's too thick and straight. Her only chance is the key, which is somewhere on Cousin Wilbur's person. He's been keeping a close eye on her all day. When she turned to the cupboard to put away the plates, he was peeking in the kitchen door. When she was cleaning Gristle's bedroom, he was watching from the hallway. As she scrubbed the bathtub to a gleaming shine, she smelled the faint whiff of orangutan fur nearby.

The edge of the bathtub is as far as the chain can reach. Tabitha can't make it to the bathroom window, let alone all the way outside, with the manacle clamped around her ankle. She counts the minutes ticking by and feels a sick, worried feeling in her belly as the sun begins to set.

When night falls, she takes the little kitchen knife she uses to peel vegetables and hides it in her waistband. Cousin Wilbur misses that small movement, but she won't manage the next part of her plan with him watching. She needs a distraction, so as she takes Bertha her before-bed slice of cake and a glass of cider, she grabs a great big pinch of salt from the salt bowl on the kitchen table and drops it into the golden liquid.

'Pthew!' Bertha shrieks when the cider touches her lips. 'Pthew! Pthack-ack-ack-ack! Someone's trying to poison me! There's poison in my cider!'

There's the smash of a glass hitting the wall and while Cousin Wilbur moves towards the noise, Tabitha takes the canister of milk from the fridge and pours it down the sink. She replaces the canister and goes back to wiping down the counter.

'Are you deaf, you slimy insect?' Cousin Wilbur roars at her from the hallway. 'Get in there and sort this out.'

'Yes, Cousin Wilbur.'

Tabitha brings Bertha another glass of cider (without salt this time), then waits for Gristle's bedtime. Her heart is fluttering in her chest all the while.

* * *

The stars are out when there's a frantic knock at the front door.

'Tabitha!' Dr Sherback's voice calls from the other side. 'Tabitha, you must hide.'

Gower flings open the door and curls his lip.

'What do you want, you wrinkled old hag?'

The doctor ignores the rude query, pushing right past Gower and into the kitchen, where Tabitha stands at the sink.

'You have to hide,' the woman says, her voice quivering. 'They're coming, adult atrociteruses, a whole herd of them. They're coming up the wall!'

There are five brilliantly coloured newts hanging off the woman's clothes, looking slightly unsettled by all the noise.

'Right now?' Tabitha says. 'Are they above the sunline?'

'Not yet,' the doctor says, 'but it won't be long. I

only managed to catch a handful of these wretched newts. They're absolutely the worst-behaved animals I've ever dealt with.'

'You're not going down there with just five newts? One of them knocked out a single baby atrociterus. Surely you'd need hundreds to knock out a herd of adults.'

'Undoubtedly, but hundreds of them won't comply. Five is all I've got, so five will have to do.'

'But Dr Sherback—'

Tabitha doesn't get to finish before the doctor is snatched from behind by Cousin Wilbur and flung towards the front door.

'You stupid ape,' the woman yells, 'there's an army of fanged atrociteruses climbing up the wall right now. You must hide, all of you, or you'll be gobbled up like popcorn.'

'What's she saying?' Gower says. 'What's coming up the wall?'

'Atrociteruses!' the doctor cries, but she is met with

blank faces. 'Monsters, you blundering oafs, *monsters*.'

'Pfff,' Gower sniffs. 'What a load of rubbish.'

'Codswallop,' Cousin Wilbur agrees. 'Now get lost and be quick about it, or would you prefer another flight to the rock wood?'

Dr Sherback backs out the garden gate, narrowing her eyes.

'Tabitha,' she shouts, 'you hide somewhere, my dear girl, somewhere safe. You know what's coming.'

Then she turns and runs back towards the rock wood with her five little newts in tow.

CHAPTER TWENTY-THREE

THE PLAN

What's all that bloody noise? Don't you twits know it's nearly bedtime?'

Gristle comes sleepily down the stairs, and Tabitha knows it's now or never. She keeps her expression as innocent as possible as Gristle fills a bowl to the brim with cereal, then walks to the fridge.

'What the hell?' Gristle says, shaking the empty milk canister. 'Who drank all the milk? What bloody eejit drank all the milk and left none for my bedtime cereal?!'

She is red-faced now and turning on Gower and Cousin Wilbur.

'Don't look at me,' Gower says. 'I steer clear of

dairy. It's mucus-producing.'

'What did you do,' she says to Cousin Wilbur, 'drink it by the pint? You greedy, selfish hairball!'

'Say that to my face,' Cousin Wilbur growls.

'I did say it to your face, you moronic monkey, I'm looking right at your ugly face.'

It's all about to get out of hand, so Tabitha cuts in.

'Please don't fight. I can get some more.' She looks to Cousin Wilbur and holds up the chain. 'You have a longer one of these, don't you? You can hang me off the edge and I'll get some more from Richard and Molly. It's dark already, but I'm sure I can find them if you swing me from side to side.'

Cousin Wilbur steps close to her and exhales foul-smelling breath from his nose. Tabitha thinks he suspects something. Finally he says, 'Fine, but make it quick. And no chatting, or I'll drop you altogether. Got it?'

'Yes, Cousin Wilbur.'

The longer manacled chain is very long indeed.

Cousin Wilbur produces it from the cupboard under the stairs, hanging loops of it over his hand and shoulder. He digs into the fur on his belly and produces a small key. Tabitha's eyes go wide. This is it. This is the moment.

She acts casual, leaning against the kitchen counter as he unlocks the manacle on her ankle. He quickly moves to replace it with the longer-chained version, but Tabitha springs into action. Poking him in the eye, she slips out of the chains and sprints around him, kicking Gower aside, who falls into Gristle, who immediately starts scrapping with her brother.

Tabitha is at the bottom of the stairs when an almighty ape roar shakes the house. She runs up the steps, hearing Cousin Wilbur's heavy breath behind her. She runs down the hallway – she's nearly there – through the bathroom door – she can see it now – leaps for the windowsill and,

'*Ugh.*'

She is on the floor and the orangutan has a hold of her ankle. Cousin Wilbur is so angry he is spitting as he talks.

'You're done for, you filthy slug trail, you hear me? I'll clamp a chain around your leg so short you're going to have to live *under the kitchen sink*.'

Tabitha tries to squirm out of his grip, but it's no use. She is caught, her plan won't go ahead, the doctor will die trying to stop the atrociteruses with five little newts, and everyone she knows will get gobbled up on the wall.

But then something happens, a wonder of nature. The wind changes.

Cousin Wilbur's face goes all skewy and he starts to shrink. His long orange hair ungrows into his skin, which turns a greyish-brown. His legs merge into a swishy tail and his arms mould into broad fins. The ape face vanishes beneath a protruding nose, which grows and grows and grows into a long, flat snout, and on both sides of the snout spring sharp teeth.

Tabitha smiles. Cousin Wilbur hasn't been a sawfish in quite some time.

He thrashes about angrily, but he's a useless fish out of water. Tabitha hops onto the windowsill. She pulls the little knife from her waistband and is about to crawl up to the roof when she has a better idea. Dropping the knife into the sink, she leaps to the floor and tucks the flailing fish under her arm.

Cousin Wilbur makes climbing to the roof more hazardous – he wriggles and squirms and swears until he's hoarse – but he's far too useful to leave behind. Tabitha stands at the very top of the green net, where the vines first sprouted. She looks down. The sunline is not clear as there is no sun, but the moonlight is enough to see quite far down the wall. She doesn't doubt that she'll see them coming. Dropping to her knees, she turns Cousin Wilbur upside down so his saw-like snout is against the vines, and she starts sawing.

There's a snapping *pop* as she cuts through each

vine. The weight of the huge net pulls on the last few strands so the whole thing creaks and complains, causing a few roof tiles to crack or go whipping off the roof altogether. There is one vine left; one vine keeping the net poised and ready to fire. Tabitha pauses and watches the wall. She is not waiting long. Within minutes she sees lumpy shadows crawling into the light of the moon. From a distance they're tiny, but she knows that up close the atrociteruses are gigantic. They're moving quickly, like black beetles scurrying up the bedcovers. Tabitha gets to work. She saws and saws as quickly as she can while Cousin Wilbur growls and swears. The atrociteruses are a little less tiny now – close enough that Tabitha can see the hint of mist that rises from their sweaty fur as they claw their way up the vine net. Her arms are tired but she saws faster and faster until,

POP, WHOOFF.

The great net falls through the night air, billowing out like a green-latticed sheet. Tabitha holds her breath. The net seems to be falling in slow motion until finally it disappears beyond the reach of the moonlight. The steaming black beetles are gone.

'Oh, thank goodness!'

Tabitha sits back and lets out a breathy laugh. A net won't hold the atrociteruses forever, but for right now, at least, the wall is safe.

'What are you laughing at, you little snotrag?' the sawfish growls at her feet. 'Wait til the wind changes. You're going to be one sorry little squashed maggot.'

Tabitha smiles and enjoys her relief while she can.

'Yes, Cousin Wilbur.'

CHAPTER TWENTY-FOUR

THE NEWT ARMY

Tabitha leaves Cousin Wilbur in the bath. When she descends the stairs Gower and Gristle stand in the hallway, both with arms folded and sporting bruises from their scrappy fight.

'That was all your fault,' Gower is pouting. 'Admit it or you'll spend the rest of the night giving Bertha a pedicure.'

'It was all my fault,' Tabitha repeats, too tired to argue.

'Where's the milk?' says Gristle.

'I didn't get it. I was too busy fending off a herd of giant monsters. I've knocked them down the wall for a bit, but they'll be back. That's why I need to leave. I need to get to Dr Sherback.'

'You lying weasel. Monsters and doctors? You absolute fibber. You were just too lazy to go get milk, too lazy by half. Well, we'll soon fix that.' Gristle grabs the long chain from the floor. 'Hold her down, Gower, til I get this thing on her leg.'

Tabitha readies herself to run, but she doesn't get the chance. The walls shake with a piercing scream from the front room. Gower snatches Tabitha by the ear before rushing in to Bertha, who is wriggling in panic on her beanbag.

'Get them away!' the woman shrieks. 'Get the wretched things away!'

'What things?' says Gristle.

'There, in the window! They stand there staring, the little maggots. Kill them, kill them all.'

Tabitha looks to the window and catches her breath. A multicoloured row of bright-eyed newts stand to attention on the sill. They are indeed staring intently through the glass. It's an unnerving sight.

'Kill them,' Bertha shrieks again, 'kill them all!'

Still holding fast to Tabitha's ear, Gower grabs a bronze figurine from a shelf and marches to the front door.

'Open it, Gristle,' he says, though his hands are shaking, 'and I'll take care of this.'

But when the door is opened, the Plimtocks gasp in horror. Standing on the threshold are more newts – all on two legs, straight-backed like soldiers – and behind the row at the door is another row, behind them another and so on all the way back to the garden fence. There's a quiet, watery sound of all those pale eyes blinking.

'Shut the door!' cries Gristle, but the newts are already inside.

They swarm up the wall on their sticky feet, down the skirting and along the floor.

'Get off me!' Gower yells, brushing at a newt that has landed on his shirt. He runs up the stairs shrieking, Gristle not far behind.

Tabitha doesn't run. An army of newts is a very unusual sight, but being a sensible girl she knows *they're only newts*. They're small and soft and they don't have sharp fangs or claws. She stands in the hallway as the newts crowd around her. One red and purple creature climbs up her leg, up her back and settles on her shoulder. Then she notices they have all stopped moving. They're standing upright again and staring right at her.

With the screaming of Bertha, Gower and Gristle ringing in her ears, Tabitha walks slowly to the door. The brightly coloured amphibians fill the garden; they're perched on the upturned metal tub where Bertha's nasty beanbag gets washed, they're lined along the washing line and the fence, and more cover the ground all the way to the pond. And still they're not finished gathering. Tabitha can see more blue and violet and pink and green little animals crawling from the direction of the rock wood.

Tabitha moves into the garden and the swarm

moves around her like a river around an island. When she stops, they stop and stare. When she moves, they get out from under her feet but stay close. Far from feeling intimidated, Tabitha finds it sort of comfortable; as if the newts and she are one being. She turns to the red and purple one on her shoulder.

'It's about time we were leaving, don't you think?' she says. 'We've got a job to do.'

Like the Pied Piper and his unfortunate child followers, Tabitha leads her army of newts back to the rock wood. It's a long walk but she doesn't feel the time go by. She reaches the opening to the secret tunnel that leads to Dr Sherback's laboratory. Just as she lifts the moss lid, a pair of gigantic, goggled eyes emerge from the darkness.

'Tabitha! Good blazes, you got out!'

'Dr Sherback, I'm so glad to see you.'

The doctor looks up from the hole in the ground and grins. 'I caught the show.'

'The what?'

'The giant vine net! The whole lot of them were tangled in it – they sailed right past me. I was chasing them from the mouth of my lab, but before I could even get close they were already at the point of the sunline – atrociteruses are awfully quick climbers, and that useless handful of newts I had were doing me no favours. Thought it was a lost cause and then *WHOOSH*! There they all go, tumbling back down in a great big net. You are a fiendishly smart individual, Tabitha Plimtock.'

'Thank you.'

'You've bought us time, you clever thing, so I made my way back here to see if I could catch any more of those troublesome amphibians.' Dr Sherback nods at Tabitha's shoulder. 'I see you've caught one already.'

Tabitha smiles. 'I've got more than one.'

With a curious look, the doctor crawls out of the tunnel and gawps at the multicoloured swarm over the rock wood floor.

'Well, stick me in a shell and call me a squiggly

limpet, that's amazing! How did you get them to stand to attention like that?'

'I don't know,' Tabitha says. 'They've gathered around me before, but I didn't think anything of it then. I don't know if they just like me or what, but I think they'll follow me to the base of the wall, if you don't mind us using the tunnel to your lab.'

'What's mine is yours, my dear girl.' The doctor stands up and holds a welcoming hand over the entrance. 'Off you pop then.'

Tabitha dives into the tunnel and hears the rush of a thousand newts following behind. They spill out onto the laboratory floor like an exploding kaleido-scope.

'Nimble little brats,' the doctor says when she arrives at the bottom of the slide, untangling a few wayward newts from her grey hair.

'So,' Tabitha says, 'what's the plan?'

'The plan is, we get this lot to the base of the wall and knock out the atrociteruses before they have a chance to regroup and re-climb. Ooh, but there'll be no hitching rides on flitter-rats this time. A whole flock of them couldn't carry this many newts, and they'd probably be inclined to gobble up the little beggars.'

'Will that be dangerous? Climbing the whole way down.'

'Absolutely. As slippery as a dishonest mermaid; the wall is slimy moss from here to the bottom.'

'It'll be worth it,' says Tabitha, 'to save everybody above the sunline. Do you think Mr Cratchley will be able to move back home afterwards?'

'What difference does it make? Can't he stay where he is?'

'Oh, but he loves his home so much; it's where he's comfortable. And he has made it so beautiful. You'd appreciate it, Dr Sherback, it's full of glowing colours. He's dressed the walls in bioluminescent algae – it's all pink and blue and green.'

The doctor starts.

'Pink?' she says.

'And blue and green,' says Tabitha.

'Yes, but pink, my dear girl, *pink* algae?'

'Yes. Why?'

Dr Sherback rubs her chin. 'That stuff grows like wildfire.'

'Oh,' Tabitha says. 'From what you said before about algae at the base of the wall, it sounded to me like the pink one was rare.'

'It is, it is, when *blue* is around. But without any competition, the pink stuff reproduces like rabbits in a hurry.'

'Is that important?'

'It may very well be,' Dr Sherback says, 'but right now we've got more urgent things to think of. Saddle up those teeny warriors of yours, Tabitha. We're about to invade the base.'

CHAPTER TWENTY-FIVE

THE INVASION

The climb down is the most difficult Tabitha has ever done. Above the sunline the wall feels like *her* wall; it's dry and rough and her fingers cling to the rock like she was born there. Near the base the wall is no longer *her* wall; it's damp and slippery and covered in moss. Her fingertips grow sore as they grip the slimy stone for dear life.

It's not just Tabitha that's struggling. The poor newts, even with their sticky feet, slide down the wall and over each other like a slow-moving waterfall. Handfuls of them have given up on the wall altogether and cling to Tabitha's jumper and trousers. The extra weight isn't helping her keep her balance.

'How come you don't keep jars of *Toadus humungus* mucus?' she asks the doctor. 'So you can get down the wall easier.'

'That stuff is only sticky when fresh,' Dr Sherback replies. Some newts are clinging to her shirt too. 'It'd go rancid and useless if I tried to keep it in the lab.'

Tabitha's whole body is tense, and her sides are hurting when the doctor finally says, 'Not long now. I can see the base.'

Tabitha looks down and wishes she hadn't. There's destruction below.

The atrociteruses landed with a bump. There is a shallow crater in the mud on the ground, and muck and shards of stone radiate out from it like a frozen splash. The vine net is in shreds (Tabitha feels a pang of regret for the trusty vines she spent her life climbing), torn apart by the monsters fighting the net and each other. And the monsters are angry. Very, very angry.

Saliva drips from their gigantic fangs as they slather

and snap at each other. The steam wafting from their sweaty fur has made the base positively foggy. This is not good news for visitors. As always, the base is viewed by Tabitha under the eerie red light of her headlamp. The red light never travelled very far, but now it's hitting patches of heavy fog and she can see nothing beyond. There's a monster (fangs, terrifying eyes, etc.), then fog, then another monster, then fog. Are there more monsters behind the fog? Probably.

'I don't like this,' she whispers.

'Well, you'd be weird if you did,' the doctor replies. 'Now I'm thinking the best plan of action would be to surround them. They're still fairly clumped together there, so we get those newts in a great big circle and—'

'Aaahhh!'

Tabitha is falling. That slippery wall has finally gotten rid of her and she is falling backwards … into a herd of angry fanged atrociteruses.

* * *

Tabitha lands with a thump that makes her see stars. Then the stars go yellow and huge and vaguely eye-shaped. Then other stars grow and grow until they are great, hanging icicles of white. Eyes and teeth, that's what she is seeing. Loads of them, all around her, looking down at her.

'Oh no.'

One atrociterus licks his giant lips. He leans in with his mouth wide – a mouth so big she'll be lost inside – and,

CRUNCH.

Another atrociterus had the same idea, and their heads crash like two buses.

They growl at each other.

They snarl at each other.

Then they leap at each other and Tabitha is in the eye of a hairy tornado.

The storm is swept to one side and another beast steps up and licks its lips. That starts another fight, but this can't go on forever. Then Tabitha has a terrible idea. She gives herself one second to come up with something better, but a terrible plan is all she has.

The front leg of the nearest atrociterus is centimetres from her head. She springs to her feet and scrambles up the leg. It's like climbing a tower. The spikes of sweaty fur are so rigid with dirt they're like ladder rungs. The handful of newts still clinging to her shirt are in the way and she nearly knocks them off as she scurries onto the top of the atrociterus's head.

'That summery smell,' she whispers to the little amphibians, 'would have come in very handy there.'

She starts to wonder if she and the doctor have made a mistake. Maybe it's just the red and purple newts that release the summery smell; maybe it's just that *one* red and purple newt that releases the summery smell.

She doesn't have time to worry further. At first the atrociterus seems perplexed by the tiny weight on his head (which he shakes back and forth), then he seems amused (he waggles his head like he is wearing a silly hat), then he seems nervous (he has noticed the other atrociteruses staring and slathering and growling at his head), and then he turns and bolts.

It's like riding a galloping mammoth. Tabitha can barely hold on. The atrociterus bounds forward on all fours, thundering to the left and then to the right to avoid the huge animals rushing at him. They come out of the dark and the fog, their teeth gleaming in the red light. Tabitha's atrociterus veers left, then left again, then left again. It's running in a huge circle. Not being the smartest creatures in the animal kingdom, the other atrociteruses are running in a circle after him; none of them think to turn in the opposite direction and catch him head on.

Tabitha catches occasional glimpses of Dr Sherback. The woman has located an enormous porcupine spine and is pole vaulting towards the stampeding herd. It's clear what she intends to do – pole vault over the leading atrociterus and swipe Tabitha off his head as she goes. Tabitha can see a million things that might go wrong with that plan. She glances at the ground, searching for a spot that might be soft enough to land on, with a place nearby to hide. But it's all muck and crater.

Looking down, however, she does see a strange multicoloured river swarming around the outside of the atrociterus circle. A thousand newts are racing along the ground like a horde of sprinters suddenly overtaking on the final stretch, and they're catching up to Tabitha's atrociterus. She is transfixed until a sudden rush of fresh air bursts from her jumper. She looks down in horror at the nervous little newts grasping her front.

'No,' she cries, 'not now! Why did you do it now?'

The smell is so odd in these surroundings; the scent of a sunny meadow down at the dark, damp base of the wall. Tabitha bobs up and down on the head of the atrociterus who is now nodding alarmingly. He stumbles, but finds his feet. He yawns and stumbles, but stays upright. Finally, the sleepiness overtakes him and he stumbles and slides to a crashing halt on his chin. Tabitha is thrown off and lands hard in a muddy puddle.

The chasing atrociteruses have slowed. They're coming towards her through the fog, panting and grinning. She smells their awful breath; it's far too hot and humid, like a rainforest. They're all around her now and there's nothing she can do. She wonders which one will get to eat her. What will she taste like? Will it be quick, with one crunching bite? Or will the monster roll her around in its mouth for hours like a boiled sweet?

She never finds out. A blast of summer air hits her almost as hard as a slap in the face. It's sensational. Her eyes are closed and she is lying in fresh, green grass, basking in pleasant sunshine with the gentlest of breezes brushing her hair. When she opens her eyes she can't believe the reality. Despite the cool, lovely air, despite the smell of a summer field, she is lying in mud in darkness, in the dankest of places.

Whoompf, whoompf, whoompf.

One by one the atrociteruses fall. They dreamily close their eyes and topple to the ground. Tabitha leaps to her feet to avoid the falling beasts. She finally makes it to the outer circle, to the moat of newts, all standing to attention.

'Not before time,' she says to them, smiling, 'but wonderful work.'

CHAPTER TWENTY-SIX

REVIVING THE WALL

When calm has settled at the base of the wall, and Dr Sherback has checked and double-checked that Tabitha is not hurt, the whole place seems wonderfully quiet and sleepy.

'The poor dears,' the doctor says, watching the snoring atrociteruses.

'*Poor dears*?' says Tabitha. 'You mean the monsters that very nearly ate us all up?'

'Of course. It's not their fault they ran out of food. If you were starving, wouldn't you chow down on a squiggly limpet or a ninja star or a ghastly mudslinger?'

Tabitha grimaces at the thought of chomping on any one of those things.

'I suppose so, if I was desperate.'

'Indeed,' says Dr Sherback, 'and we've made these animals desperate. But that's something we may be able to put right.'

Dr Sherback shows a sudden desire to meet Mr Cratchley and visit his home. The swarm of newts, as if reading Tabitha's mind, remain at the base, emitting further blasts of summery air any time the monsters start to twitch and yawn themselves awake.

In his wall pocket, Mr Cratchley stands at the doorway nervously wringing his hands as Dr Sherback scrapes pink algae from the walls into large jars.

'We'll have to take it all, alright Mr Cratchford?' she says.

'It's Cratchley,' Tabitha says. 'Are you sure it's alright with you, Mr Cratchley? I know it's a big change.'

'I know you wouldn't ask, Tabitha,' he says, 'if you

didn't really need it. So yes, please take it all.'

His words say he's fine with it, but Mr Cratchley's shaking body and trembling fingers tell Tabitha that he finds losing his pink light dreadfully upsetting. His watery eyes watch every scrap of algae as it is scraped away from the rock. Tabitha would take his hand if physical contact didn't make him uncomfortable; instead she stands very close and watches with him, to let him know she understands.

'This stuff is going to do marvellous things, Cratchley,' Dr Sherback says as she whips another lump of algae into a jar. 'Maybe even save the world.'

'I've been meaning to ask,' Tabitha says, 'how is it going to help?'

'Well, re-growing enough blue and green algae at the base could take a number of years, so the pink stuff is going to be a stop-gap. Remember how I said it grows like wildfire when it's got no competition?'

'Yes.'

'So I dunk a load of this at the bottom of the wall

and – thanks to the nourishment your wonderful shredded vine net will provide – this stuff is going to spread like … well, like wildfire. Squiggly limpets aren't fussy eaters, so they'll chow down on the pink algae and then they'll start reproducing more. Which means the ninja stars will have more to eat and they'll start reproducing more, which means–'

'Which means there'll be more ghastly mud-slingers, more skunkified werbles, more slimy flitter-rats–'

'And on and on until the populations have recovered. By that time the blue and green algae will have set themselves up nicely, they'll take over and we'll have that lovely blue-green-with-a-hint-of-pink balance again.'

'But won't there be a lot more atrociteruses?'

'Yes, but my dear girl,' Dr Sherback says, 'they'll have enough of their natural food source down there, so they won't be forced to do weird things like climb the wall in search of foodstuffs they wouldn't normally eat. Hey presto, the world's a wonderful place to be again.'

'That's a brilliant plan!' says Tabitha.

'It is,' says the doctor, 'but it only works on two conditions.'

'Which are?'

'Number one, your army of newts keeps the atrociteruses subdued until the pink stuff can get a foothold.'

'I think they can manage that.'

'And number two, that people change how they're doing things up there.'

'How do you mean?' asks Tabitha.

'Detritus, girlie. The algae at the base of the wall must get fed by the plants at the top.'

'Oh, right, yes.'

'And in order for that to happen, the edge of the world can no longer be a dusty, rocky hell. We've got to bring back the greenery, get planting. And when things get growing we've got to take care of them sensibly. No more using up things so they can't grow back. Moderation, my dear Tabitha, that's the key. Understand?'

'I do.'

Though Tabitha feels sure her relatives won't.

* * *

As it turns out, Tabitha never discovers how the Plimtocks feel about Dr Sherback's plan. The house at the edge of the world is empty. Apparently the newt army was more than Gower, Gristle, Cousin Wilbur and Bertha could handle. Their clothes are gone, as is the last of the food from the fridge, and even Bertha's stench-ridden beanbag. All that's left behind are a few dozen wayward newts who missed the battle but have comfortably set up home in the empty house.

Tabitha strolls through the rooms, enjoying the peace and quiet. With a glowing smile she gently